The Nem̶...̶ ̶C̶e̶l̶l̶

The Nemesis Cell

Brian L Porter

Dedication

The Nemesis Cell is dedicated to the memory of my mother, Enid Ann Porter (1914 – 2004), whose love and support never failed me, and to my wife, Juliet, who supplies those commodities in our everyday lives together.

By the Same Author

- A Study in Red – The Secret Journal of Jack the Ripper (*Winner, The Preditors & Editors Best Thriller Novel Award, 2008*)
- Legacy of the Ripper
- Requiem for the Ripper
- Pestilence
- Behind Closed Doors
- Glastonbury
- Purple Death
- Avenue of the Dead
- Kiss of Life

Novelette

- Dracula Doesn't Live Here Anymore

Short Story Collections

- The Voice of Anton Bouchard
- A Binary Convergence (with Graeme S Houston)

As Harry Porter

- Tilly's Tale
- Dylan's Tale
- Wolf
- Alistair the Alligator

Acknowledgements

The Nemesis Cell began life as a short story. One of the first to read it, Sheila Noakes, enjoyed it so much she wanted to know more about the characters, and encouraged me to develop the story into a full-length novel. Writing the longer version has proved to be an enjoyable experience, for which my thanks go to Sheila. She has also read each chapter as it has been completed to ensure that the new version lost none of the attraction she felt for the original short story.

The character of Harry Houston is based largely on the help and information provided to me by Detective Chief Inspector David Moffat of the Scottish Police College at Tulliallan in Fife. His assistance has been invaluable in developing Harry Houston as a person and as a police officer.

Malcolm Davies has read and re-read *The Nemesis Cell* so many times he probably knows it better than I, and I thank him for his time and efforts in ensuring that the story remained fluent and concise.

To Graeme S. Houston I owe my thanks for his superb cover designs for both the e-book and the paperback versions of the book, and his encouragement along the way. For finding a home for the print version, my gratitude goes to my agent Aidana.

Finally, as always, my thanks go to my dear wife Juliet, for her patience and her support through the long hours she has sat alone listening to the sound of my fingers upon the keyboard. Her honest criticisms help keep my writing on the straight and narrow.

.

Part I

A NEW GENESIS

Prologue

Spring 1974, Ostend, Belgium

The woman screamed, a primeval howl that represented the un-changing nature of humanity's physical continuance through the ages. Though she'd promised herself she wouldn't no matter how great the pain, she had finally given in to the most natural urge associated with the birth of a child, and, at the moment the head finally forced its way from the birth canal and made its way slowly into the world, her body could take no more. She'd heard that scream so many times in the past, from others in the same position, and had thought those women weak and incapable of self-control. Now, she knew better.

The man in the white coat whose hand she gripped tightly spoke gently to her, reassuring, coaxing. "It won't be long now, it will soon be over, and all will be well."

She was sweating; her legs ached from being held apart for so long by the stirrups. He'd insisted on them, in case he needed to take immediate action if complications developed, and her back felt as though it would never again be free of pain. Over and over in her head she asked herself if anything was worth the pains and the humiliating exposure she was enduring, and over and again the answer came back to her. Of course it was!

As the man had promised, it *was* soon over. The pain gradually subsided, and the woman, free at last of the weight she'd carried within her womb for so many months, and with the pain of childbirth receding into memory, slept. The man sat watching her contentedly, knowing that between them, they had achieved something special, perhaps as all men who witness the birth of a child feel, though this was more than special, and he knew it. He had no idea of what the future might have in store for any of them, but for now, he basked in the glow of success as he watched the sleeping woman's breasts heave gently beneath the thin gown as she breathed rhythmically in her deep, well deserved sleep.

Darkness fell over the small isolated cottage, the sound of the ocean waves breaking on the nearby beach. The man checked one last time that his charges were happily sleeping, and as a combined sense of relief and elation crept over him, he finally succumbed to the tiredness in his limbs, his eyes slowly closed, and he too drifted into a peaceful sleep. There was much work to do; it would take time, patience, and much trial and error. But that could wait until tomorrow.

Chapter One

Turin, April 1976

The news from around the world had hardly been good. On the 2nd April of that year, Prince Sihanouk of Cambodia stepped down as monarch of his country in the face of the rising tide of communism that had taken hold of the land, to be replaced by Pol Pot, who became Prime Minister, and virtual dictator of that beleaguered nation. Few people could have envisaged at that point the holocaust that would soon sweep across Cambodia, killing millions and bringing fear, degradation, and sweeping poverty to almost all who dwelt within Pol Pot's evil sphere of influence.

Whilst the happenings in South-East Asia were serving to make headlines around the world, news of lesser global proportions but of intense personal importance were the chief topic of speculation at the home of Antonio and Lucia Cannavaro, where news of paramount importance had arrived.

"The letter, Antonio, I've got the letter, from the clinic. I've been accepted!"

"*Cara, cara,* I'm so happy for you, for us, my beautiful wife. Maybe now we will be able to have the family we have longed for."

"Yes, my husband, and they will pay us well for allowing me to let them use their new methods upon me."

"As long as it is safe, then I am happy, my darling. Please, may I see the letter?"

Lucia passed the letter to her husband, who began to read.

The Clinique Sobel

Brussels

28th March 1976

+32 (0)2 640 97 97

Dear Signora Cannavaro,

I am delighted to inform you that, following your application to the clinic, and the subsequent results of the tests carried out by our representative in Turin, it has been decided to offer you a place on our experimental infertility treatment programme.

As was made clear at your local interview, you will be required to spend a period of two months with us, during which time we will apply a revolutionary technique developed by our medical team to bring an end to your infertility and hopefully to ensure that you and your husband will be blessed with a child of your own in the near future.

At the end of your time here, you will be paid the agreed sum of two thousand dollars to recompense you for the time you will spend here and to compensate for the separation from your husband.

At all times during your stay here, we will adhere to safe medical practices and you will at no time be in any danger of harm. As was also pointed out to you at your interview, however, the practices we employ are revolutionary in the field of medicine, and it is necessary that you do not reveal your participation in these trials to anyone outside of your immediate family, and preferably then only to your husband.

Your failure to adhere to these conditions will invalidate this offer to participate, and your place will be offered to some other fortunate lady.

Please be kind enough to telephone the above number at your earliest convenience to confirm your acceptance of this offer, and please follow this with your signed acceptance.

Congratulations once again on your success, and I shall look forward to making your acquaintance when we see you at the clinic on May 1st.

Yours sincerely
Charles DeVries
Dr. Charles DeVries
Administrator

Antonio and Lucia danced around their tiny apartment together. They were far from wealthy, Antonio making just enough for them to live on from his job as a motor mechanic at the small service garage down the street. He and Lucia had been trying for a baby since they were married three years ago. Tests had shown her to be highly unlikely ever to conceive naturally because she had a small blockage in her fallopian tubes. Further, Antonio had been found to have a very low sperm count, so their chances of a natural conception were minimal.

The tiny advertisement in the local newspaper had seemed like a message from God to Lucia. The new clinic had recently opened its doors to the public, and they were seeking women with clinically diagnosed infertility to take part in trials of their new treatments for the problem. They promised a high chance of success, and even to pay those accepted for their time.

Lucia had been delighted to be invited to the office of a local doctor who had been appointed by the clinic to ascertain her suitability for the project, and had attended all the necessary and at times invasive tests required by the clinic. The doctor had sent his report to the clinic and now she had the letter, and she was happy, happier than she'd felt for a long time. Antonio shared in that happiness with his wife, dancing once more round the tiny, cramped living room of their one-bed apartment, where they both hoped soon to hear the sound of a baby's voice to join with their own.

"We shall have to buy you some new clothes for the journey, and for your stay in Belgium," said Antonio.

"We cannot afford such extravagance, Antonio," replied his wife. "We must save our money for the time when the baby comes."

"*If* it is a success," Antonio cautioned her, trying to be realistic about their chances.

"Oh, it will be, my darling, I just know it will be," she replied.

Over the next week, other couples across Europe and in the United States received similar letters of acceptance, and the delight of the young Italian couple was reflected in the joy and the excitement experienced by those fortunate enough to have been selected. At that moment, Doctor Charles DeVries, administrator of the pioneering new infertility clinic set in the heart of one of Europe's oldest cities, could have asked for and been granted anything in their power to give by those young people, such was their gratitude at receiving this opportunity to become parents.

They of course couldn't know that DeVries himself would have little or no part to play in the actual treatment they received at the clinic. He was after all just the administrator of the facility, but he did enjoy being the public face of the clinic, and he worked hard to cultivate his image as the benign and caring father figure of the establishment. Every visitor to the facility commented on his ability to put the most nervous of patients quickly at ease.

In a matter of weeks, women from around the globe began their journeys, by air, by sea, and by train to the revolutionary new clinic, where for all of them the one hope was to see their dreams of motherhood being turned into reality.

Chapter Two

The woman gazed down at the two toddlers happily playing on the floor in front of her. The two boys were perfect, almost too perfect, she thought. It was so hard to distinguish them from one another. Never had there been such twins, she thought to herself, and she had carried them within her body, had given birth to them, and now she was responsible for every minute of their daily lives. They loved her, they depended on her, they interacted with her in a way she would never have thought possible at one time in her life. They had begun to talk a few months ago, and both had the ability to walk unaided for quite a number of steps. She was proud of their progress. They had lively, active minds, as she'd always known they would have. After all, one need look no further than the man who sat in the office on the other side of the playroom wall, the man who had been by her side through the whole process, who had held her hand as she gave birth to the boys, and whose blood and genetic makeup flowed in the veins of the two boys upon whom so many futures now depended. His mind had been a part of the blueprint that had made them.

The door to the playroom opened, and the white-coated man entered and walked across, then positioned himself on the sofa next to her.

"They look well," he said, with a knowing smile on his face.

"Of course they're well, they're always well, aren't you, boys?" she replied, voicing the purely rhetorical question in the direction of the two playing children who patently were not about to provide an answer.

"Is everything going according to your childrearing programme?" asked the man.

"You make it sound so clinical," she responded.

"Isn't that what you are, a clinician, and one of the best in your field, I might add?"

"Yes, of course. It's just that they have no real conception of how important they are to me, or to you."

"One day they will know, and they will be proud of their heritage, their upbringing, their lineage."

The woman appeared to lapse into deep thought for a minute or so, and then she rose from the sofa and beckoned the man to follow her. As they retreated to the far side of the room, the twins rose in perfect unison, steadied themselves on their young legs, and began to walk slowly but surely, with an assurance rare for such youngsters, towards the couple. As they neared the smiling couple, the boys reached out with their hands. First the man, and then the woman responded in kind. The two boys took the hands of the adults, who led them into another child-oriented, cheerfully decorated room where the boys were soon sleeping peacefully under the warm coverings of their purpose-built beds, which were fitted with an array of monitoring equipment. It was time for their afternoon nap.

After ensuring that the boys were safely asleep and that the cameras that recorded their every movement were switched on and operating correctly, the man and woman left the room, retraced their steps across the pastel blue carpet of the playroom, and made their way into the office which lay on the other side of the wall.

The man stood for a long time gazing out of the office window, as the woman sat making notes at the desk. He watched a family of blackbirds as they fed upon the lawn, mother, father and two fledglings hunting for juicy worms. Next came a squirrel as it ran down the trunk of the tall tree in middle of the lawn, anxious to find a new source of food and return to its secret hideaway.

The man was lucky to enjoy such sights, for the office window was perfectly positioned to observe the small wonders of nature that were regularly taking place in the expansive garden outside. In sharp contrast to his panoramic view, in the beautifully decorated, centrally heated bedroom to which the twins had just been led, and in the superbly equipped and well-lit playroom he and the woman had just left, there were no windows at all.

Chapter Three

Brussels, May 1st 1976

"Welcome, ladies, I bid you welcome. My name is Doctor Charles DeVries, and it is my pleasure on behalf of all the doctors and staff here at the clinic to wish you all a happy stay in our facility and an even happier future upon leaving us. If you will all please give your first names to Angelique here at the desk, one at a time please, she will allocate your rooms to you and you will be shown to them directly. Remember, first names only, please, ladies. We like to preserve our clients' privacy here at the clinic, even from one another, so we make it a condition of your stay here that you only use your first names when conversing with each other. No surnames here please, ladies, ever!"

This last was delivered with such force and conviction that some of the women assembled in the foyer of the clinic that day felt as though they'd just entered some kind of strange military boot camp and that they were being addressed by the sergeant major of the rookie platoon, rather than being checked into a fertility clinic on the outskirts of the beautiful city of Brussels by the otherwise charming and extremely handsome Dr. Charles DeVries.

Each of the six women present in the spacious, brightly lit reception area of the clinic had arrived that day, according to pre-arranged instructions from Dr. DeVries. Some had arrived in Belgium, one, two, or three days ago, but had arranged accommodation in various hotels until the time had come for them to report to the clinic. It was certain that every one of them had been impressed as their respective taxis had carried them from the small local station on the outskirts of the city to their destination, and they'd observed the broad sweeping lawns of the facility as they drove up the twisting gravelled drive, which crunched satisfyingly under the tyres of the cab. The gardens bordering the lawns were lush and beautifully landscaped, with a dazzling array of flowers of every imaginable hue set in the expansive borders, a true delight to behold.

Everything about the approach to the clinic spoke of peace and serenity, of harmony, and of a place to relax, take things easy, and enjoy. There were other women already at the clinic. The new arrivals saw them taking walks in the grounds and enjoying the spring sunshine, seemingly without a care in the world. This was truly set up to be a haven of tranquillity, a place where they could forget the pressures of home, and concentrate on the one thing that mattered most to them at this time in their lives. It would be true to say that each of those six women felt as though she had arrived at a crossroads in her life, and that the new direction she was about to take would shape a whole new optimistic future for her and the baby she hoped would be hers before too long.

Lucia Cannavaro was the first of the women to reach the reception desk, her Latin temperament causing her to rush to be 'numero uno' when it came to checking in and being allocated her room. It wasn't rudeness, but it was Italian-ness!

"My name is Lucia," she stated clearly to Angelique, the receptionist, sticking strictly to the first name rule.

"Ah, yes, Lucia, you are in the Blenheim Wing, room number four," said Angelique, after checking a list on the desk in front of her. Aged about twenty-four, with blonde hair cut to her shoulders, Angelique was a highly professional medical receptionist. She was also a registered nurse, as was evidenced by the shoulder flashes on her crisp, white uniform, and the badge identifying her nursing orders stitched to her dress above the left breast pocket, from which a number of pens and a mini-torch projected, all neatly arrayed like soldiers in a row.

"Please take a seat, Lucia, and when I have allocated rooms to all of the other ladies, I will have each of you escorted to your accommodations."

Lucia did as she was bid and settled herself into one of the comfortable armchairs which were placed strategically around the reception area as Angelique efficiently continued her work with the others. As she waited, she listened as the other women identified themselves to the receptionist:

"Katerina," said the first, in an accent Lucia couldn't place, followed by "My name is Theresa," this time in an unmistakeable Irish accent.

Angelique wasted no time in assigning the two women to rooms one and three, in the same wing as Lucia. It transpired that all the women would be housed in the clinic's Blenheim Wing, this being reserved for those undergoing the newest experimental treatments and procedures.

Katerina and Theresa soon joined Lucia in the waiting armchairs, as first an American named Tilly, then an English woman by the name of Elizabeth and a Slavic-looking girl who went by the name of Christa each registered themselves with Angelique and were allocated their rooms. It seemed that each woman would have a private room during their stay at the clinic, as Dr. DeVries quickly explained that it was necessary for certain procedures to be carried out which needed privacy, and it was thought that the clients at the clinic would feel more at home if the procedures were carried out in the more homely confines of their accommodations rather than in the more clinical conditions of the laboratories or treatment rooms as used for some of the more routine fertility treatments on offer at the facility. Each and every room, he stated, was fitted with all the medical machinery and equipment necessary to carry out every aspect of their treatments, and if it weren't for the need for fresh air and exercise, they could actually spend their whole time at the clinic in their rooms, without ever seeing the daylight, though, as he laughingly pointed out, that would be like a prison sentence, and not at all what they had come for.

Some of the women giggled nervously at his words. Some, Lucia included, felt a slight shiver of trepidation as he spoke, as though the good doctor was not quite as convincing as he could have been. As soon as Angelique had finished with Christa, she pressed a button on her desk. A minute later, as if by magic, a door in the panelling behind her slid open and a man in white jacket and trousers appeared. The automatic door had opened in such silence that his entrance took them all by surprise, and drew one or two gasps from the waiting women.

"Automation, the technology of the future, ladies," said DeVries, sensing their incredulity.

Of course, today we accept automatic sliding doors as an everyday appliance as we enter shops or offices, but, back in 1976, such things were a novelty, and usually confined in most peoples' minds to those scenes in *Star Trek* where the Captain or crew member approached a solid wall which suddenly sprang open with a whoosh to allow access to the bridge or another deck of the Starship *Enterprise*. The small group of women viewed the revelation of the automatic doors as though they were indeed entering the realm of science fiction.

The young man, who introduced himself as Marc, was no Captain Kirk, but was in fact the medical orderly in charge of escorting the women to their rooms in the Blenheim wing. DeVries spoke once more.

"You ladies will now be allowed two hours in which to settle in to your new accommodation. I trust you will find everything to your satisfaction. We wish you to be comfortable here. Please, take some time to refresh yourselves, take a shower, unpack, and perhaps phone your husbands to inform them of your safe arrival. At the end of the two hours I will visit each of you in turn to discuss the direction your individual treatments will take. You are all unique; your conception problems are individual and will require one-on-one consultations at all times during your stay at the clinic. Today is all about assimilation and tomorrow you will meet the clinical team who will carry out the actual procedures that we hope will be successful in helping you fulfil your dearest wishes."

Lucia thought him one of the most considerate men she'd ever met. His voice was clam and reassuring, and she felt confident that she'd made the correct decision in responding to the advertisement.

With that, Marc bade the women follow him, and he led his multi-national cortege of ladies to their new homes away from home, in the Blenheim Wing, or 'Special Procedures Unit' as the staff at the clinic described it.

Chapter Four

In the windowless bedroom, the two boys woke and lay happily and quietly staring at the brightly coloured mobiles that dangled from the ceiling above them. In the absence of any natural breeze or draught in the room, the dangling ornaments moved almost imperceptibly, driven by the small natural currents of air produced by the breathing of the children and the ultra-quiet air conditioning system. There were representations of elephants, gazelles, lions and deer, a giraffe, and an ostrich, all of which captivated and gripped the boys' attention. Unlike other children who perhaps might cry or make some sound on waking with no adult in the room, these two were silent, doing nothing more than stare like automatons at the brightly painted creatures suspended in mid-air above them.

The woman entered the room, looked down at them with a distinctly professional air, and stood making notes on the clipboard she carried in her left hand. Her notes completed, she walked across the room, placed the clipboard on top of the chest of drawers which stood by the wall, and peered at her reflection in the mirror which was positioned just above the chest.

What she saw pleased her. She was a good looking, some might even say beautiful, woman. About five feet two, her figure had soon returned to its normal shape after having given birth to the twins. She'd taken some time to apply her make-up today–she had a business meeting later–and she was pleased with the results. Together with the dark red skirt suit she'd chosen for the day, and the heels, not too high, but enough to give her legs the desired shape and contours, she felt very feminine, but also very confident. Surely the money men wouldn't turn her down.

Returning to the boys, she picked them up one at a time, and placed them in a standing position on the floor, one at either side of her. She took them by the hand, and led them to the playroom, where the man in the white coat sat waiting.

"They're all yours for a couple of hours," she said, "I'll be back as soon as I can."

"Good luck," the man offered as she walked through the door, into the office, where there were windows, and light, and a connecting door to the outside world.

"Huh," she replied. "Luck doesn't come into it. When he sees what I've got he simply has to say yes."

With that, she was gone, and the man turned to the two little boys, who stood obediently in front of him, like two tiny statues. He ordered them to sit on the floor, and, despite their tender ages, they responded immediately. He then proceeded to read to them from a book he had kept beside him on the sofa. This was no children's storybook from which he read. It was Gibbons' *Decline and Fall of The Roman Empire.*

Chapter Five

The Clinique Sobel, later the same day.

Lucia Cannavaro was spellbound by the size and luxurious nature of the room in which she found herself. "Mamma mia," she said to the empty room, "this is bigger than our apartment at home. What would Antonio think?"

The room was indeed large by anyone's standards, and represented the extensive expenditure on its clients' comfort that the clinic had invested in its accommodations. The walls were covered in soft-hued pink and white wallpaper with a delicate floral design woven in, and the carpet, in a matching shade of pink, had a deep pile that bare feet sank into easily. Recessed lighting had been installed in the walls, obviating the need to turn on the overhead lights, which themselves were housed in an ornate solid brass fitting reminiscent of something normally found in the world's finest hotels. Obviously, whoever had funded the building of the clinic had spared no expense, and this in itself gave Lucia a degree of confidence in the venture she had embarked upon. Dr. DeVries's one small slip into his sergeant-major veneer was soon forgotten.

The bathroom which adjoined Lucia's living and sleeping space was equally palatial. There was a shower, something Lucia had only dreamed of back home in Italy. The bath itself was twice as large as the one at home, and there was also a bidet, something she had only seen in copies of expensive women's magazines on her rare visits to the hairdresser or perhaps the dentist. The whole room was finished in a peaceful tone of blue, which, though initially cold on the eye, soon gave one a feeling of restfulness and tranquillity. That, thought Lucia, was the essence of the clinic, tranquillity. Everything was designed to be harmonious, to put the client or patient at ease, and she felt that they'd done a good job; in fact, a great job!

She kicked off her shoes, and allowed herself to stretch out on the double bed. Such decadence! At home Lucia would never have the time or opportunity to lie on the bed in the daytime. There was always so much to do, washing, cleaning, ironing, making sure Antonio's meal was ready when he came home from work. Suddenly, she'd been transported to a land of immaculate luxury, and she was determined to enjoy every minute.

It was only as she relaxed that Lucia began to study the room in more detail. Against the far wall, under the window with its pretty beige curtains, was an array of medical equipment, all of it totally unidentifiable to her degree of knowledge. There were machines that looked like alien contraptions from outer space; cold, clinically designed things in stark white, in complete contrast to the soft pastels of the rest of the room's décor. Beneath one of them was a shelf, and the instruments housed on that shelf looked to Lucia's untrained eye like implements of torture. She could only speculate as to their purpose. She knew without a doubt, however, that some, if not all, of those shiny metal and plastic tools would be used on her, or in her, in some way, and her previous air of peaceful tranquillity was instantly replaced by a sense of dread, a fear of the unknown.

In an effort to cheer herself up, she forced her eyes to look away from the cold and clinical side of the room, and allowed herself once more to take in some of the more pleasant aspects of her accommodations. There was a television in one corner, a television larger than any she'd ever seen. She turned it on; the picture was in colour! Lucia was entranced. Back home in Turin she and Antonio had a small black and white TV, with a screen that was so small they had to sit close to it to make out the picture clearly. This was almost like being at the cinema, though of course she couldn't understand a word that came from it. Everyone on screen was speaking Belgian, or Flemish, or whatever it was they spoke in this country. Still, she could enjoy the wonderful clear picture.

Next to the television was a small bookcase. She skipped across the room to examine the contents. Now the attention to detail by the clinic was evident once more. All the titles on the shelves were in Italian. How thoughtful, she thought. If she couldn't understand the words of the television, at least she could read in her own language. She suddenly realised how clever the people here were. All the women who had arrived today, herself included, had knowledge of English, and the clinic had stated in their advertising that only women with an ability to speak that language would be accepted. All the staff had spoken in English today, so that would be the common denominator, the language of choice for all those who came to the clinic.

Lucia was grateful to her teachers, and the fact that she'd paid attention in school. It had been a difficult language to learn, and she'd thought she'd never grasp it, but she'd persevered, and now, today, here she was, in Belgium, all alone, speaking English to a bunch of people she'd never met before.

Isn't life strange, she thought. *Here I am, in a beautiful place like this, and me, just a simple girl from the back streets of Torino. Why, I'm even starting to think in English, too,* and she laughed out loud, a girlish giggling kind of laugh, that betrayed her underlying nervousness.

Seating herself in one of the two armchairs provided for her comfort, she looked at the bed again. The thought came to her that she would be sleeping alone that night, for the first time since her wedding to Antonio. Suddenly she was incredibly homesick and she missed Antonio terribly. How would she cope for all these long weeks to come? She thought of his strong, muscular arms, the rough hairs on his chest, and the way he would hold her so close at night, his breathing and hers becoming almost as one as their bodies intertwined, and how they would drift off to sleep in a tangle of arms and legs and dream peacefully together until morning. Yes, Lucia was missing Antonio, and the missing and the longing would only grow stronger as time went by, she was sure of that.

Just as she felt a lump rising in her throat and she was about begin to sob with the feelings of loss at being apart from her beloved husband, there was a knock upon the door. She quickly took a deep breath, pulled herself together as best she could, and strode across the room. She grasped the ornate brass door handle, turned it, and pulled the door towards her. She hadn't realised how fast the time had passed since she'd entered the room. Standing at the entrance to her room was Dr. DeVries, with a clipboard in one hand and a large file with Lucia's name printed on the front tucked under the other arm.

It was time to begin!

Chapter Six

An hour later, Lucia felt as though her brain was swimming. It had been almost impossible for her to assimilate all the information that Dr. DeVries had attempted to impart to her. Bad enough that they were conversing in English, not the first language for either of them, although he was obviously fluent, but the use of so many technical and medical terms was for the most part nothing more than mumbo jumbo to her.

As DeVries left her room, she sat on the edge of her bed and tried to make the best sense she could of the things he'd told her. At least, she thought to herself, she appeared to be in good hands. He'd gone through the reasons for her infertility as diagnosed previously, and had explained that because of her special circumstances (she still wasn't clear on what those circumstances were), she was an ideal patient for the new treatment that had been devised at the clinic. All she knew for sure for the moment was that the next day she would have her first consultation with Doctor Dumas, the clinic's senior clinician and the person who would be overseeing the special treatments that Lucia was to receive. DeVries had reassured her that all the procedures she would be subjected to during her stay were absolutely painless, and directed towards the sole aim of helping Lucia to become pregnant. The samples of her husband's sperm provided some weeks before and kept in a cryogenic facility at the clinic had been tested and refined according to Dr. Dumas's instructions, and were ready for use at twenty-four hours' notice. Dr. DeVries was reassuringly cheerful and optimistic that Lucia and her husband would soon be the proud parents they both longed to be.

If DeVries had said nothing more than that, Lucia would have been happy and prepared to undergo whatever was necessary in order to achieve her goal of motherhood. As she heard the doctor's footsteps receding down the hall towards the next client on his list, Lucia relaxed and let her head rest gently on the pillow. She'd been told that, apart from dinner that evening, her time was her own. She could stroll and explore the gardens, walk by the lake behind the clinic, or enjoy the recreational facilities provided for the patients' use. There were many diversions available for her and all the visiting clients of the Clinique Sobel, even a library stocking a multitude of books in various languages and Dr. DeVries had encouraged her to make use of them. Once again he reiterated that she should not divulge her surname to any of the other clients during any recreational activities, for the sake of her, and the other patients' privacy, he said.

She could of course choose to rest and relax in the privacy of her room, and for her first night away from home and her Antonio, that was just what Lucia decided to do. She made sure her door was locked, not from any sense of fear of being interrupted but from in-bred modesty, and then she slowly undressed, carefully folded and hung her clothes in the very large built-in wardrobe, and tripped lightly into the bathroom, where she luxuriated for half an hour in the shower. As the warm water cascaded over her body, she found herself staring down at her figure, her flat belly, and her long, lithe legs. She tried to imagine herself with the swollen tummy that would announce to the world the imminent arrival of her first-born child, and she allowed herself to daydream for a while. She emerged feeling refreshed and decided to put her feet up until it was time to dress for dinner. In the meantime she switched on the wonderful large colour TV, and, dressed in just her bathrobe, she propped herself up on her pillows, and watched an unintelligible but quite visually amusing comedy movie starring a host of stars completely unknown to her. She would phone Antonio as agreed the next night at his mother's house, as they themselves didn't possess a telephone.

In the other rooms throughout the Blenheim Wing, Dr. Charles DeVries went through the same procedure with the other new arrivals, all of whom probably felt exactly as Lucia did, a little unsure of the details, but reassured by his words and his charm. The little group of new arrivals showered or bathed, or phoned home. Some read a book, some walked by the lake or in the grounds. For many of them, it was like being on holiday. For a couple of them, being at the clinic was an exercise in asserting their right as women to bear children, and their visit and their treatment was thus akin to a sort of Holy Grail for them. They were very different in many ways, those six women who now relaxed as they awaited their first meal at the Clinique Sobel, and yet, in the most fundamental way of all they were the same. They each ached deep in their hearts to bear a child of their own, to love, nurture and raise as a part of themselves, a living monument to the love they each shared with their respective husbands.

At precisely seven thirty p.m. that first evening, Lucia Cannavaro stepped through the door of her room into the beige-tiled corridor of the Blenheim Wing. The walls were painted a faintly lighter shade of beige, and were hung with prettily framed prints of old masterpieces, Turners, Vermeers, Da Vincis, and Van Goghs. With fluorescent lighting built into the ceiling, the overall effect was one of peace and light. They seemed big on that in the Clinique Sobel, thought Lucia. She was joined in the corridor by the Swiss girl, Katerina, who emerged from her room at almost the same moment as Lucia. Together they followed the signs that led them to the dining room, where they and the others would have their first real chance to converse together since their arrival.

They were the first ones there, though they were quickly joined by the others. Any thoughts Lucia may have had about having a free and easy discussion with her fellow patients was soon dispelled when Dr. DeVries and Angelique swept through the doors and greeted the women warmly. Clearly, they were not to be left alone for dinner. It was as if the doctor, or someone else perhaps, didn't quite trust them to keep their names or origins a secret as they'd been requested to. What better way to ensure that than by a degree of supervision? At least, that's how Lucia thought of it at first. In the event, there would be plenty of time ahead for the women to talk. When that time came, strangely perhaps, no-one broke the clinic's strange code of ethics with regard to revealing their full names.

The meal itself was sumptuous by Lucia's humble standards. With avocados stuffed with fresh North Atlantic prawns to start, followed by fillet steak served just as each woman requested it, and followed by a selection of the finest desserts and sweetmeats she could ever remember seeing, Lucia felt as though she were dining in the Ritz, the Dorchester, or one of the other grand hotels around the world she'd previously only read about, or seen in movies. The meal was served with a choice of still or sparkling spring water; alcohol was banned for the duration of their stay. There was coffee afterwards though, the most wonderful tasting freshly ground coffee Lucia had ever drunk, served with little chocolate mints, a nice touch again, she thought.

During the meal, she took the opportunity to look more closely at her dinner companions. There was Dr. DeVries of course, who, now he'd dispensed with the professional white coat and was dressed in a casual white shirt and grey trousers, looked more like the male lead in a daytime soap opera. He was very handsome, thought Lucia, and probably younger than she'd imagined when meeting him for the first time. Lucia had an in-built respect for persons in authoritative positions, which made her mentally add about ten years to their ages. To Lucia, great responsibility went hand in hand with age, like the priest at home, or her own doctor, who looked seventy but in all probability was much younger.

As for the other women at the table, Angelique aside, she now noticed something she'd missed earlier. Apart from different lengths and styles of their hair, and slightly differing facial features, they all bore something of a resemblance to each other. Dark hair, brown eyes, similar build and height, and all were about the same age. Perhaps, thought Lucia, it was something to do with the treatments; only women of certain physical characteristics were suitable. Her theory was foolish, of course, as she quickly told herself, but, in reality, it wasn't too far from the truth. Lucia wasn't to know that of course, nor did the others. They never would.

The presence of DeVries and Angelique having acted to stifle the conversation slightly, the meal passed in almost total silence, with the doctor himself doing most of the talking. Oddly, although he talked a lot, Lucia felt that he didn't really *say* much. His conversation was bland, giving away little about the medical intricacies of why they were all assembled here in the clinic. He mentioned that in addition to Doctor Dumas, they would also be meeting Doctor Renaud, who was the Director's chief assistant, and who would be doing much of the actual work involved in the ultimate process of insemination when the time came, under the supervision of Dr. Dumas. As for Angelique, she was a cosmetic addition to the assembled diners, a feminine presence to represent the clinic at the table, nothing more.

Before she finally laid her head down to sleep that night, Lucia gazed at the photo of Antonio she'd placed beside her bed. Missing her husband very much, she reached out, took the picture in her hands, and kissed the rugged handsome face that smiled out at her from within the brassed frame. Then, gently placing Antonio's likeness back on the bedside cabinet beside her, she lay back, closed her eyes, and was asleep in minutes.

Chapter Seven

The woman studiously watched the two boys at play. The puzzles she'd provided for them were almost complete, and she allowed herself a smile. Two years old and yet so clever! She took an intense pride in their achievement in completing the exercise. She hadn't thought them quite ready for such an intellectual challenge, but they'd surprised and delighted her with their display of manual and rational dexterity.

She looked around the room, taking in the aura of the peaceful and aesthetic surroundings they'd created for the children. The lack of windows had no effect on the boys, of course, for they'd never seen a window, and therefore had no concept of what one was, or what it was for. They'd seen pictures of the outside world–that was a necessary part of their primary education–and it would soon be time to take them outside for the first time, but not yet. When that time came they would take them together, perhaps for a walk in the forest, where they could observe the boys' first interaction with the natural world and their general surroundings. First, of course, there was much work to be done. If their planned exercise in educational techniques was to work, the boys must continue to develop and learn as they were already doing. Windows, and the obvious distractions their presence would cause, had no part to play in that plan.

Their game finished, the two boys looked up at the woman and smiled. She was always amazed at how broadly they smiled, not the typical smile one would expect of a two-year-old, more the knowing smile of an educated man, one who knew he had just achieved something extraordinary. She smiled back, and looked toward the one-way mirror on the wall. He would be there of course, in the office on the other side of that wall, observing, as always.

"Be good boys now, won't you?" she grinned at the two children happily playing together on the floor. "Mama and Papa have some more work to do. Be good, lie down on the cushions, sleep a little, be good."

Be good seemed to act as a kind of trigger to the two toddlers. They quickly moved to the pile of cushions in the corner of the room, and obediently lay down, closed their eyes, and in seconds both were dozing happily.

"They're doing really well." said the man in the office as she entered and closed the door behind her, locking it automatically.

"Like two beautifully trained lap dogs," she replied.

"Really, I think you could use a better analogy than that."

"Why? Didn't you see how they responded to the sleep command? How many two-year-olds will do as they are told in such a way?"

The man sighed and looked again through the mirror at the two beautiful little boys lying peacefully and contentedly on the cushions in the corner of the light, bright, windowless room.

"Really well," he sighed, "they're doing really well."

Chapter Eight

The Clinique Sobel, the next day

Lucia woke, bright and refreshed, at seven a.m. She'd slept well, despite the absence of Antonio by her side. She guessed that the journey to the clinic had taken its toll on her resources and caused the overwhelming tiredness that had sent her into her long dreamless sleep. The mild sedative mixed into the food she'd eaten the previous night was of course unknown to her, as it was to all the women. It was the clinic's policy to ensure that all their clients had a good night's sleep on their arrival, and the sedative was routine, but of course it was considered by the director that the women needn't know it was being administered.

She showered, and then, as she was about to select which of her three dresses to wear that morning, she allowed her bathrobe to fall from her shoulders, and she studied the reflection that gazed back at her from the full-length mirror attached to the inside of the wardrobe door.

Reasonable pretty, (so she thought, modestly), her hair still wet and plastered to her head, with a slim figure, Lucia smiled as she tried once again to envisage her flat belly growing larger, her hips swelling, and her breasts filling out with the tell-tale signs of impending motherhood. She wondered if Antonio would still find her attractive with her figure distorted by the life that she hoped would soon be taking shape within her body, and she knew instinctively that he would. The baby wasn't just Lucia's dream; it was something that both of them wanted more than anything in the world, and her husband, who worshipped the ground she walked on, would love and care for her as no other man could if she were to become pregnant with his child. As she slid her hands slowly down her body, ending at her hips, she smiled once more, selected the white dress with the floral design at the neck and hem, and soon dressed and made her way to the dining room once more for breakfast.

Breakfast was a casual affair, with all the residents of the Blenheim Wing present as at dinner the previous night. There was no Dr. DeVries or Angelique, and the women all displayed a certain air of relaxed informality without the clinic staff present. There was more conversation than at dinner, and the women soon began to open up a little with each other, though they stuck to the confidentiality rule as before.

The American, Tilly, introduced herself to the others in a slightly nasal New York drawl.

"My name's short for Mathilda, but no one *ever* calls me that. I hate it. My parents named me after my paternal grandmother who happened to share the same birthday as me, or me with her, whichever way it should be. She died a year before I was born so I guess it was their way of commemorating her. Yuck. I'm a waitress in a diner, not great work, I know, but, hey, it's steady and the pay ain't bad. My husband, Vincent comes of Italian stock, so hey, Lucia, we have something in common, huh? He works in a meat processing plant, and boy, does he stink when he gets home from work, but what the heck, I love the guy, right?"

One by one, the other women gave each other a brief biography of themselves.

Elizabeth spoke next. The English girl was the same age as Lucia and had an almost identical figure. They could have been sisters, but they weren't, of course. Elizabeth, like Lucia, didn't actually work herself. Her husband Michael earned a moderate wage from his work as a baggage handler for the London Airport Authority, and they lived modestly in a small apartment near Gatwick Airport. The Irish girl, who had introduced herself as Theresa, was something of an enigma to the others. She was a little younger, and seemed afraid of her own shadow. There was a nervousness about her that seemed out of place, even allowing for the unusual circumstances of their presence at the clinic. Recognising a good Catholic Irish girl, Lucia suspected that Theresa had something to hide, though she was certain that the girl would have been thoroughly checked out by the clinic before being offered a place on the programme.

Theresa *was* afraid, but not of anything she was to encounter at the clinic. She and her fisherman husband Patrick had spent many hours in conversation with Father Donnelly, their priest back home in Ireland, and he had made his disapproval of any artificial means of achieving pregnancy quite clear to them. They had promised him that they would never do such a thing, hadn't confessed to responding to the clinics' advertisement, and then, as the clinic insisted on such secrecy about the programme, had told him she was going to visit her aunt in Liverpool to cover for her time here in Belgium. The series of lies lay heavily on Theresa's mind. She pondered long and hard on the consequences of lying to her priest. All in all, she was terrified that despite her wish to have a child to call her own, if Father Donnelly were to find out what she'd done, he would call on God to visit his wrath upon her, and on Patrick, and that they would both suffer the fires of eternal Hell.

Lucia knew nothing of this, though she would probably have sympathised with the Irish girl's ethical and theological dilemma. She and Antonio had no such fears or worries. Despite being Catholic themselves and living as they did in Italy, close to the heart of world Catholicism, they had avoided any such disapprobation by not speaking to their priest at all on the subject of her infertility. That, they had long ago decided, was their own personal business, and any conflict with the will of God would be resolved in private between them and their Maker.

Katerina was from Zurich, and her husband Wilhelm worked as a watchmaker. She was extremely pretty, though a little shy and nervous, and didn't really offer much in the way of personal information about herself.

Finally, the girl with the Slavic features, who had introduced herself at the desk the day before as Christa, told them a little about herself. She wasn't Slavic, but came from a village outside the Polish capital Warsaw. She and her husband Peter had escaped from behind the Iron Curtain of communism some years before and now lived in a small country town in Germany, in the heart of the beautiful Bavarian countryside. She spoke fluent English, German, and Russian in addition to her native tongue, but it was hard to find work in Germany for a Polish émigré of any description, and it was important for her and Peter to maintain a low profile. He had been an aircraft engineer at home, she explained, but now worked in a local garage, mostly repairing tractors for the local farming community. They had tried for a long time to have a chid of their own, and now, she explained, with tears on the brink of falling from her eyes, they saw this as her last chance for motherhood, and to raise a child born free of the yoke of the communists, in the new home they'd made for themselves in the free west.

Lucia felt an enormous sorrow for Christa, though she thought also that there was much in her story that she wasn't telling to her and the other women in the room that day. Few people escaped from behind the Iron Curtain that had drawn a veil over the freedom of so many nations now in thrall to the Soviet Union. None of the Warsaw Pact nations took kindly to defections, and few ordinary people would have the necessary contacts or financial muscle to enable an escape to the west to be organised. So, though she felt an affinity for the woman, and wished her well, Lucia felt that she should hold a little of herself in reserve during any direct conversation with the Polish girl.

After all, weren't they always being told that there were communist spies everywhere? Perhaps Christa was one of them, sent to pry into the clinic and its methods. Lucia thought that this was probably a preposterous idea, but nevertheless, she would be careful around Christa.

As two attendants cleared the breakfast table, the door to the dining room opened, and a cheerful and smiling Charles DeVries entered the room.

"Good morning, ladies," he intoned, "I hope you all slept well. Please don't hurry yourselves. There is plenty of time before your meeting with the Director. Perhaps you may like to take walk in the grounds, it's such a beautiful morning, or relax in your rooms for a while. Doctor Dumas will be here at ten, and would like to speak to you all in the main lounge at that time. She will hold personal consultations with you later in the day, of course, but to begin with she wishes to give you all a general overview of what you can expect during your stay with us."

Lucia didn't feel like walking in the grounds. Instead, she returned to her room, where she sat on the bed thinking about all she'd heard that morning. For the most part, the other women were very much as she was, ordinary, respectable married women who were quite simply desperate to have a child of their own. None were wealthy, that much was certain, so perhaps the clinic had a policy of helping those who were not in a position to pay vast sums for fertility treatment, as she'd heard was possible in the USA and some other nations. After all, she thought, why should someone be able to virtually buy a baby or a pregnancy at least, just because they had the money to pay for the treatment?

At that moment, satisfied that she'd answered her own question, and answered it well, Lucia was immensely grateful to Dr. Dumas, Dr. DeVries, and everyone connected with the Clinique Sobel. These were indeed good people, and she was glad of that. It made her feel safe to place herself in their hands, for, as she thought to herself shortly before making her way to the main lounge some time later for her meeting with Dr. Dumas, these people really cared!

Chapter Nine

"Endometriosis," said Doctor Margherita Dumas, "is one of the chief causes of female infertility. In this condition, as you ladies are probably already painfully aware, the tissues which normally line the uterus grow outside the uterus and attach themselves to the organs in the abdominal cavity, such as your ovaries and fallopian tubes. Eventually, bleeding leads to scar tissue which can lead to blocked fallopian tubes or interfere with ovulation. It is a progressive disease, and the treatments available are not necessarily guaranteed to either cure the disease, or to allow for normal impregnation to take place. In short, some, though not all of you ladies suffer from this condition, and it is our fervent wish, through the use of my new and unorthodox techniques, to bring to you the chance to have a child of your own despite the presence of the disease."

With every eye in the room upon her, and in an atmosphere where one could have heard the proverbial pin drop, Dumas continued.

"Some of you have what is termed PCOS, or Polycystic Ovary Syndrome, one of the most common causes of infertility. The leaflet that Doctor DeVries is handing out now will explain this in more detail for the benefit of those affected by it. There are of course other ovulatory disorders which may contribute to your inability to conceive naturally, and these will be explained to each of you as appropriate during your personal consultations with either me or Doctor Renaud, whom you will meet shortly. I think that concludes the lecture for the moment, ladies, except for me to say that I wish you all a happy, restful, and successful stay with us. My staff will do all in their power to make you feel at ease and at home here at the clinic. I, for my part, will endeavour to ensure that you leave here with at least the opportunity to make your own personal dream come true."

At that, a round of spontaneous but polite applause broke out around the room. The women had just heard everything they had needed to hear from Doctor Dumas. Forget the technical medical jargon, she had once again offered them the chance to achieve their ultimate goal, that of becoming a mother. At that moment, nothing else mattered to them. This was where they wanted to be, where everything would happen for them, and they saw Margherita Dumas as little less than a saint. This woman, young and quite beautiful herself, seemed to know exactly was in the mind of each of the women who sat in the comfortable chairs in front of her. She knew how to reach them, how to talk to them, and perhaps, most importantly to the women themselves, she seemed to know how to help them!

As the applause died away, Dumas smiled expansively, and spread her arms wide as if to embrace the women in the room.

Thank you," she said appreciatively, "but such displays are not necessary, I assure you. I am here to help you, and you are here to help me. Without your co-operation in agreeing to be the first group to undergo my highly specialised and revolutionary procedures, the work of the clinic, and the chance to help hundreds, perhaps thousands of women like yourselves would be lost. The rest of the medical world have tried hard to stand in the way of progress for years when it has come to the subject of infertility, but we are on the verge of a great breakthrough, and you are part of that breakthrough. Remember, though, the contracts you have signed. Whatever happens here, and whatever the results of your treatments may be, you must remember that it is vital you keep the fact of the special treatment to yourselves. When the time is right, it will be acceptable for you to admit to having received help in treating your infertility, but that, ladies, is as far as it goes. Is that completely understood?"

There was a general murmur of assent from the women in the room. Though they may not have been sure of the reasons for the secrecy, the general feeling amongst the gathered assembly was most definitely one of the ends justifying the means. Lucia herself thought that she knew why the doctor needed to keep things to herself. Clearly, the doctor's procedures had not received the nod of agreement from the medical authorities, and were probably therefore technically illegal, but, what the hell? If it worked she would bless the doctor's name in her prayers until her dying day.

As the meeting broke up for coffee, served by the same two young women from breakfast time, another man entered the room. None of the women needed telling that this would be Doctor Renaud, Margherita Dumas's number two at the clinic. Lucia, Elizabeth, and the others had to stop themselves from staring. Without doubt, Doctor Alexander Renaud was one of the handsomest men they had ever seen. He was a veritable Adonis, six feet tall, his shock of dark hair cut in a fashionable collar-length style, and his hands seemed more like those of an artist than a surgeon. Then again, some of them thought that a good surgeon was very much like an artist, his hands being the tools of his trade, required to move and perform with a sensitive touch. Perhaps his most striking feature were his eyes, deep cobalt blue, and with a warmth that the women felt could probably melt the coldest heart. Doctor Renaud was, to put it in the common idiom, a hunk, and they couldn't wait to make his acquaintance.

Renaud spent the next five minutes speaking to Dumas, casting an occasional glance towards the new arrivals, smiling and nodding in the direction of anyone who managed to catch his eye.

As the coffee cups were cleared away, and the women resumed their seats, Doctor Dumas once again addressed them.

"Ladies, may I introduce Doctor Alexander Renaud? Doctor Renaud is my senior assistant, and a major shareholder in the Clinique Sobel. He is as anxious as I am that your stay here will be a happy and a mutually successful one. I will now ask him to say a few words, after which we will leave you to rest and relax until after luncheon, when we shall visit each of you in the privacy of your rooms to discuss your individual treatments."

When he spoke, the women's first impressions of Doctor Renaud were confirmed. His voice simply reinforced the impression created by his appearance. The American girl, Tilly, thought his voice something like that of the American actor Tom Selleck, soft, yet deep and sensual at the same time.

"Good morning ladies," said Renaud. "It will be my pleasure to assist Doctor Dumas and yourselves in the great adventure on which we have all embarked. Nothing will give me greater pleasure than to see each and every one of you leave here with the prospect of imminent birth on the horizon. Together we shall work towards that goal, and I will endeavour to make each stage of the process as simple and as comfortable for each of you as is humanly possible. Although you are unsure and hesitant about some of the things that will happen here, I can assure you that everything will be done with your safety and comfort in mind. No risks will be taken with your health, or with that of your potential offspring. I promise you that you will be in safe hands here at the Clinique Sobel. On that you have my word."

Every woman in the room felt like swooning. It was as if they'd been addressed by a demi-god, such was the hypnotic and reassuring tone of Renaud's voice. Any lingering doubts any of them may have had about having agreed to becoming guinea pigs for the wonderful new treatments on offer at the clinic were dispelled in the few moments it had taken for Renaud to deliver his welcoming address.

The meeting ended with many smiles and a feeling of optimism and anticipation amongst the women, the clients of the revolutionary Clinique Sobel.

Lucia and the others couldn't resist a look back into the room as they filed out. It was a delight just to feast one's eyes on the delectable form of Doctor Alexander Renaud, and like giggling adolescent schoolgirls, they all wanted one last look, even though they knew they would be seeing him again, very, very soon.

The women returned first to their rooms. Then Elizabeth went for a walk in the grounds, enjoying the peaceful contrast with hustle and bustle of home. She was joined by Tilly, also enjoying the tranquillity, so different from her home in New York. Theresa visited the communal lounge where she sat by the large picture window, reading a magazine until she began to do off, and she dozed happily for a while as the sun shone through the glass pane, warming the room beautifully. Christa kept to her room, not wanting to mix too closely with the others. She had an in-built wariness around strangers; a result of her upbringing under the repressions of communist rule.

Lucia stayed in her room as well, though in her case, she put her feet up on the bed and watched a rather inane game show on the television, once again in a language she couldn't understand, but at least she could enjoy the frolics and silliness of the contestants.

Time passed quickly. Soon it would be time for lunch, after which the individual consultations would begin, and the next stage in their quest to become mothers would be underway.

Chapter Ten

In the windowless room, the two infant boys slept, blissfully unaware of the cameras that watched their every move. The only sound in that room was the soft but incessant whirring of the air conditioner, which constantly recirculated and scrubbed the air that the children breathed day in and day out.

The sound of a key turning in the lock of the door that connected the room to the office was too quiet to disturb their sleep, and neither of them stirred as the woman entered the room. Walking across to where they lay, she slowly and quietly removed every single plaything that had been in the room before they'd fallen asleep. When they eventually awoke, they would be totally alone, save for each other, and their overwhelming urge would be to cry for their mother. There were no teddy bears to cling to, no mobiles hanging from the ceiling, and, apart from the cushions on which they lay, no furniture remained in the room. The woman had removed the sofa and the chair earlier.

Their sense of physical deprivation should be all that was needed to create the perfect bond of reliance on her that she needed to create. They would trust her, love her, comply with everything she wished them to do, and at the same time, they would learn. They would learn faster, with greater accent on detail than any child in the accepted mainstream systems of education that existed all over the world. She would turn them into geniuses. She would prove that her theories could work.

Leaving them to sleep a little longer, the woman returned to the office and reviewed the pictures recorded by the cameras for the last few hours. She wanted to analyze every second of the last few hours, and she had notes to write up.

Education? What did the so-called experts know?

The air-conditioning whirred, the boys slept, and the room echoed to the tiny, restful sounds of their breathing.

Chapter Eleven

Aberdeenshire, Scotland, May 1976

As Lucia Cannavaro began the first of the treatments intended to cure her infertility, a birth was taking place a long way from the clinic that would have a bearing on the futures of all the women in the Blenheim Wing of the Clinique Sobel, though no-one would have known it at the time.

In the midst of the Scottish countryside, in the tiny village of Torphins, stood a quaint and rather beautiful building that went by the name of the Kincardine O'Neil War Memorial Hospital. The hospital was in fact a very small maternity unit, which fell under the auspices of the Aberdeen Royal Infirmary some thirty miles away. With just five beds and a small staff, the unit existed to provide maternity facilities for some of the more isolated communities in the region.

So it was that at about three-twenty p.m. on a Tuesday afternoon, Mrs. Margaret Houston gave birth to her son, who she and her husband Angus would subsequently name Hamish, a good old Scottish name, though one which would lead to some light-hearted ribbing and banter as the child grew up. 'Hamish Houston' just had a certain ring to it.

Margaret Houston remained in the unit for four days, walking her new born son in the grounds when the weather permitted, in a pram provided by the hospital, and, as a very special service, almost unknown in maternity care in major hospitals at that time, the staff at the unit allowed Angus Houston to take his wife out for a meal and a few precious hours alone on the night before they took the young Houston home. It was something the staff at the hospital had done for a long time, and due to the small number of births it actually catered for, the babysitting service caused absolutely no disruption to the routine of the staff, and was always appreciated by the new mothers and fathers who took advantage of the generous offer.

Kyoto, Japan, May 1976

Upon his return from Belgium, Ichiro Tanaka sat in his palatial office on the top floor of the building that housed the headquarters of the corporation that bore his name. What he'd seen in Ostend had convinced him to invest heavily in the woman's project. Tanaka was shrewd; a businessman with an eye to the future, and what she'd showed him had given him a vision of that future. He was still young enough to be certain of enjoying the vast financial returns on the project well into the next thirty or forty years, so the short-term financial drain from his personal fortune would be well compensated for by future returns on his investment. Only Hoshiko Yamagata, his personal secretary, was aware of his dealings with the woman, and it was a tragic loss to the corporation some weeks later when both Tanaka and poor Hoshiko were killed in a freak accident on the freeway when Tanaka's limousine was hit by a large chunk of falling masonry as they passed under a flyover in the process of construction. Tanaka's driver, who also died in the accident, lost control of the car, and the three of them were killed when the vehicle careered across three carriageways of traffic and shot over the parapet of a bridge into the river below. Back in Ostend, the woman heard of the deaths on the international business news programme on the TV, and she received the knowledge with a resigned sigh and a smile. She had all the investment she required and no one would ever come asking for the money back!

At the subsequent inquiry into the deaths it was discovered that there had also been a fault in the braking system of the limousine, and that upon hitting the murky waters of the river, the door locks had jammed, making any escape impossible. A verdict of accidental death by drowning was returned on all three victims.

Chapter Twelve

Clinique Sobel, June 1976

May had given way to June. Lucia and the other women in the Blenheim wing had all undergone numerous treatments for their individual problems with Doctors Dumas and Renaud. Their initial heady excitement at being involved in the project had given way to a resigned boredom with the innumerable procedures and tests to which they were subjected. The weeks of being poked, prodded, and having various medical instruments inserted into the most intimate parts of their bodies had turned into a daily routine that most of them now wished would end soon, so that they could return home to their husbands.

Most kept in touch with home by phone, or letter, or both. Lucia wrote mostly, only being able to phone Antonio at certain pre-arranged times, when he would be waiting for her call at his mother's house. Though they missed each other terribly, they both looked forward to the time, soon, when their dreams would be realised. Doctor Dumas had virtually promised it would happen, and they accepted her word without doubting her for a moment.

Only one event cast a cloud over their stay. During the first week of June, Christa had received word from her mother that her husband Peter had been killed in a terrible accident, when a tractor engine had fallen from the pulley it was attached to and had struck him a fatal blow on the head. Before leaving the clinic in tears for her home, Christa had begged of Dumas to be allowed to return after the funeral, to have her husband's sperm used to inseminate her so that she could still give birth to their child, in order that she would always have something of her husband to remind her of the man she loved. Doctor Dumas had been sympathetic, but adamant. It was the clinic's policy only to enable a child to be born into a family comprising a married mother and father, thus enabling the child to enjoy as stable and conventional an upbringing as it was possible to guarantee. None of Christa's tears or entreaties would move her. The doctor remained implacable.

All the women in the Blenheim Wing of the Clinique Sobel had joined in the overwhelming wave of sorrow that was expressed to the poor Polish girl, who eventually left in a cab on a warm sunny morning, her face a mask of tears as she waved her final goodbyes to them, the Clinique Sobel, and all her hopes for the future. As the cab disappeared down the long gravel driveway, Lucia said a number of prayers, for Christa, for the soul of her dead husband, and one of thanks for God's gift to her of the husband she loved and adored and who was waiting patiently for her at their little home in Turin. Finally, she asked God to grant her the gift of the child that she so craved, and ended with one for the doctors and nurses of the clinic, that they might be successful in their attempts to procure that eventuality. She crossed herself, and watched the cab as it shrank to a tiny blot in the distance, finally disappearing around the bend in the drive, as it carried its tearful cargo of sorrow to the railway station.

Later, she was to speculate that perhaps her theory that Christa and her husband had been political refuges on the run from the communists in their homeland had been correct. Maybe Peter had been the victim of an assassination by agents of the Soviet Union, or the Polish Government. Christa had said he'd been an aircraft engineer at home in Poland. Perhaps he'd been trying to sell military or aviation secrets to the West, and they'd killed him to prevent what the communists would have seen as his treachery. Would Christa be safe on her return to Bavaria, or would they seek her out also and kill her too?

Lucia smiled to herself as she thought how preposterous her theory would sound to Antonio, or to anyone else for that matter. It had been an accident, a tragic one certainly, but had Christa's own mother not told her it was so? Lucia knew that Antonio would accuse her of having read too many paperback thriller novels, the sort she often bought second-hand at the local market, and which she would eagerly devour, before selling them back to the dealer for a few lira, and then buying yet more of the same.

Even Antonio would have been surprised therefore to learn that two members of the Polish Legation in Germany were expelled from the country some weeks later, having been accused of 'activities not conversant with their roles as diplomats', the universal governmental jargon used when expelling those thought to be spies or other undesirables travelling and living under the guise of diplomacy. Lucia and the others of course would never hear of the circumstances that really surrounded the death of Christa's husband, as, once she'd left the clinic, they never heard from her again. They would have been shocked to learn that just six weeks after her husband's death, Christa's shattered body had been found on a railway line not far from her home. It was thought that in the midst of her grief at the loss of her husband she had jumped from a bridge into the path of an express train, and had been killed almost instantly.

Back in Brussels, Lucia was excited as Doctor Renaud entered her room.

"So, Lucia, here we are again," said the doctor in that quiet calm voice that so inspired confidence in his abilities from all the women. "The good news is that the egg we implanted with your husbands sperm has fertilized exactly as we hoped it would, and we are ready to begin the implantation into your womb. If all goes well, Lucia, you will leave here pregnant!"

"Oh, doctor, yes, please, I'm so happy. Please tell me what I must do."

"Please lie on the bed, Lucia. The procedure will take only a short time, as have all the others. There is nothing to worry about, you will barely feel a thing, I promise."

All over the Blenheim Wing that day, Doctor Renaud made his rounds, reassuring the women and carrying out the final phase of the procedure perfected by Doctor Dumas. All of the women were delighted to have reached this stage of their treatment, and the atmosphere in the rooms and the corridors of the Wing was almost something that could be touched. This was, after all, what they'd all come here for.

After completion of the implantations, Renaud instructed the women to rest for a while, and avoid any strenuous activity, even walks in the grounds, for the rest of that day. He ended each consultation by verbally inviting each of the women to dinner with himself and Doctor Dumas that evening in the dining room. It may have been delivered with charm, and in a voice that was as inviting as could be, but all the women knew without a doubt that this was an invitation that could not be refused.

As she lay resting in her room, gazing longingly at the photograph of Antonio by her bed, Lucia could think of nothing other than the fact that already, perhaps, new life was beginning to take shape within her body. She placed her hand on her belly, imagining a stirring in her womb. Foolish girl, she thought to herself, but she didn't remove the hand.

This could have been the most important day of her life, she decided, and it was certain that similar thoughts were flitting through the minds of the others at that same time. Christa might have been a million miles away at that moment. Sadly, as far as the women in the Blenheim Wing were concerned, they had matters of supreme personal importance on their minds and, for all their previous feelings of sympathy towards her, the Polish émigré had ceased to exist for them from the moment her cab had disappeared from their view. The reality of her subsequent death would become a matter with which they would never be disturbed.

Chapter Thirteen

"Tick, tock, tick, tock." The two little boys sat close together, talking in unison as the second hand on the Mickey Mouse wall clock revolved around the cartoon character's face. The woman smiled and watched them as they gazed attentively at the passing of the seconds. She pointed one by one at the numbers on the clock face and listened as the boys clearly enunciated "one, two, three," etc.

"And who is this?" she asked, pointing at the face in the centre of the clock.

"MICKEY," the boys shouted out together, their smiles an indication of their pleasure at the interaction with their mother.

"My, aren't you my clever little boys?" she continued. "Now, I want you to listen very carefully."

At that, the woman began to read to them, as the man had done previously, from a book not normally associated with children as young as two years old. This time it was Jules Verne's *Twenty Thousand Leagues Under the Sea.* The two little boys listened attentively, their faces were identical masks of concentration. She knew that they would learn more from this exercise than they would by looking at stupid picture books such as were normally given to children of their age. She didn't expect them to remember what she was reading to them in any great shape or form, but she knew that they were assimilating words, sentence constructions, and vowels, all of which would aid them in their development. They might not have a mental picture of the *Nautilus*, or the giant squid, but when they eventually saw a picture of a squid they would remember it from the book. Let them know the words first, and add the visual interpretation later, that was her philosophy.

After reading to them for half an hour, the woman rose and walked to where the boys were sitting. She patted each of them on the head, as someone else might pat a puppy for being good, and took each boy by the hand, leading them into the bedroom, where she instructed them to lie down and sleep. Without a murmur, they obeyed her command, and lay down quietly on their beds, still smiling as though happy and satisfied to have pleased their mother. As she walked from the room, the woman thought that, if they'd had tails, they would have been wagging them now!

As the door closed, the room fell silent, except for the ever present whirr of the air-conditioning, and the boys looked at each other, and as one, in that quiet windowless room, they began to chant in their babyish sing-song voices,

"Tick, tock, tick, tock, one, two, tick, tock, three, four, tick, tock…"

Chapter Fourteen

Ballater, Scotland, 1976

Angus and Margaret Houston had been inundated with visitors almost from the moment they'd arrived home with young Hamish. Uncles, cousins, and grandparents in addition to dozens of friends and neighbors had maintained a constant stream of visits to the couple and their newborn son in their home not far from the royal castle at Balmoral.

Here in the highlands of Scotland, the young Houston would have the perfect start in life, surrounded by a loving family, with the benefits of fresh air, magnificent scenery, and a first class education. It was known pretty much throughout the British Isles that the Scottish system of education was far superior to the systems in operation in England, Wales, or Northern Ireland. In those early days at the family home, Angus Houston was quick to tell anyone who would listen that his son would doubtless follow him into the family business. Angus was a butcher, a very good one at that, and owned a shop in the village of Ballater that he was proud to say had provided fresh meat for more than one great banquet up at the castle. He hoped (and would one day see his dream realised) to see the Royal Warrant displayed above the door to his shop, identifying him as an official supplier to Her Majesty the Queen.

On the day of the baby's baptism, performed in the local Church of Scotland by the local minister Daniel McFadden, it was Angus's brother Daniel Houston who coined the name which was to stick with the younger Houston for the rest of his life. Despite the name of Hamish having been given to him by his parents, and the child having been christened with that name in the house of God, Daniel walked up to Margaret, held out his arms to receive the child and said, "Come on to your Uncle Daniel now, young Harry."

The name had stuck there and then, and despite the protestations of his parents, the family and all of their friends seemed to prefer the name to that given to him by his mother and father. So, on the day he was accepted into the family of God, Hamish Houston also became Harry Houston, a name that would one day be held in high regard by many folk in his native land.

Houston the elder, butcher first class, would, at some time in the future, have to look elsewhere in his family for someone to follow him into the business, as young Harry was destined for other things in this world.

It was one of the hottest summers on record in the United Kingdom that year, and the young Harry Houston enjoyed almost perfect unbroken sunshine during his first few months on Earth. From his lively demeanour and busy little hands, it was evident from the start that the young lad was going to be intelligent, and his mother lost no time in making sure everyone knew just that.

At sea, British and Icelandic ships, naval and civil, squared up to each other in what became known as the Cod Wars. In Uganda, Israeli Special Forces launched a successful rescue mission to free the hostages held aboard an Air France Airbus at Entebbe, and the USA celebrated its bicentennial. Harry Houston, just a few weeks old, knew none of this, but these, and other events around the world from that day forward would do much to shape his future, and the ultimate direction his life would take. For now though, he was content to gurgle happily, eat, sleep and drink, and feel contented as he was gently rocked back and forth on his mother's knee. Margaret Houston was a loving, doting mother, and her little boy would never want for love and affection as long as she was around!

Chapter Fifteen

Ostend, Belgium, Summer 1976

"Won't they feel disorientated when we take them outside for the first time?" asked the man.

"It's possible," replied the woman. "But I think the time is right to try it."

"One each?" was his next question.

"One each," her reply.

A few minutes later, the man and the woman led the two boys by the hand from the playroom and through the usually locked office door. The boys made no sound, but their eyes took in every detail as they walked across the office towards a door that the two of them had never seen before.

The man unlocked the outer door, opened it, and a shaft of sunlight filled the room through the opening. The boys gasped in admiration at the sudden explosion of light; it was unlike anything they'd seen before. Without further hesitation, first the man, and then the woman, led their charges through the door and out into the sunlit garden. It was the first time the boys had been outside in the fresh air in their lives!

The twins looked all around the garden, saying nothing, taking in the sights, sounds and smells that assaulted their senses. They took deep gulps of the sweet fresh air that now filled their young lungs.

There was no sign of the disorientation the couple had feared. Instead, one of the children suddenly stopped in his tracks as the man led him along, pointed upwards to the branch of a tree, where a male blackbird was perched, and said,

"Papa, look, bird."

"Good boy, Alexei, yes, it's a bird," said the man, who then turned to the woman and asked her, "How the hell does he know it's a bird? He's never seen a picture of a bird in his life."

"You see," she replied, "It works, the system works. He may not have seen one before, but he's heard birds described in the books we've read to them. He instinctively associated the various descriptions in the texts he's heard with the creature he sees in the tree. It proves you don't need to see something in order to know what it is. Like a blind man, he might not know what a diamond looks like, but put one in his hand and he'll likely tell you it's a diamond. I knew it. This means that everything we've done has been a success. We can continue to educate them in this way and they'll continue to learn at a rapid rate, far faster than in the conventional education systems of the world."

Suddenly the other boy pointed in the direction of the bottom of the garden.

"Mama, I can hear the sea."

"You see," the woman shouted at the man, "What did I tell you?"

"Incredible," said the man. "I wouldn't have believed it if I hadn't seen it with my own eyes."

"Now do you believe me?" she asked.

"Absolutely!" he replied.

"Come Arturo, come Alexei, we shall show you the ocean," said the woman.

Together, she and the man led the boys to where the garden sloped away at the cliff edge, and the two boys gazed together at the blue-grey waters of the North Sea, their first view of the ocean. Far away, just on the horizon, they saw an oil tanker slowly making its way to port. Nearer, a flock of seagulls swirled over the waves, seeking fish to catch. The boys identified everything they saw.

After a half hour, the woman decided that enough was enough for their first expedition into the outside world and she brought the session to an end.

Before leaving the edge of the cliff, Arturo and Alexei looked down once more at the beach and the open vista of the North Sea that stretched away into the distance and the boys smiled in excited admiration at the moving, swirling waves below them, and giggled with happiness.

"We must go back now," said the woman, and she and the man led the two little boys back through the garden and into the house, where they were soon back in their air-conditioned windowless playroom.

"We go outside again one day, Mama, please?" asked one of the tiny tots.

"One day, Alexei, one day," replied the woman as she left them once again to their own devices in that brightly lit, highly functional soulless room.

"They'll soon be asleep," she said to the man when she returned to the office. "Make sure the cameras are running before we leave. We'll go into town and feed them when we get back. The fresh air will have given them an appetite."

The man gazed through the one way mirror, and, sure enough, the two boys were curled up fast asleep on the pile of cushions in the corner of the playroom. The couple made sure all the doors were locked as they left the house for their trip to town.

The air-conditioning continued its incessant whirring in the room where the boys slept, dreaming of things they had yet to see.

Chapter Sixteen

Clinique Sobel, June 1976

Lucia's time at the clinic was at last coming to an end. All the procedures scheduled had been carried out, and she and the other women
were waiting for confirmation from the doctors as to whether their
treatments had been successful. As she waited in her room for her next
meeting with Doctor Renaud, she couldn't help thinking about the
future, of all the wonderful times ahead for her and Antonio, if only
they could be blessed with a child. She made mental pictures of the
three of them playing in the park together, of perhaps getting a puppy
to grow up with and play with the child, of Christmases spent listening
to the happy sounds of a child opening gifts.

She wanted to be at home now, with Antonio. She'd been here in
this foreign country long enough. Belgium was nice, but it wasn't Italy,
it wasn't Turin, and despite the luxurious surroundings of her room
and the facilities at the clinic, Lucia was missing her little apartment,
her husband, her daily life. As she waited for Renaud to appear and
give her the news she wanted so badly to hear, Lucia closed her eyes,
and allowed her mind to transport her to her home, and she could
almost smell the aromas of the street where she lived, the spaghetti
being cooked in the neighbouring apartments, the diesel and petrol

fumes rising from the street outside. She was definitely suffering from a bad case of homesickness.

There was a knock at the door, followed by the voice of Doctor Renaud.

"May I come in please, Lucia?" he asked through the door.

"Yes, doctor, please do," she called.

A smiling Alexander Renaud strode into the room, and Lucia instinctively knew that the news was good. Unable to contain herself, she jumped up from the chair and grasped the doctor by the arm.

"Doctor Renaud, please tell me, you look so happy, it is good news, yes?"

"Lucia, please calm yourself, you'll make yourself out of breath, and that would never do for a lady in your condition, now would it?" he replied.

"My condition? What do you mean, my condition? Wait, doctor, are you saying…?"

"Yes Lucia, that's exactly what I'm saying. The latest tests show that the procedure has been successful. The implantation of your husband's sperm into your egg led to fertilisation, as you know, but the big test was whether your womb would accept the artificial implant. I'm pleased to tell you that it has, and as of this moment, you are officially pregnant."

Lucia clasped her hands together in delight. Despite herself, she threw her arms around the doctor's neck and planted kisses on both of his cheeks. She was deliriously happy.

"I don't know what to say," she said breathlessly, her excitement growing by the second. "What do I do now, doctor? I mean, is there anything else I need to do here at the clinic, or, can I go home to my husband?"

"Lucia, my dear," said Renaud, trying to calm the over-excited young Italian down. "You must stay here for just a few more days. Then, when we are satisfied all is well, you can go home to your husband, and the pregnancy will continue along normal lines. You will need to check in with your doctor at home from time to time, and you will have our telephone number in case of anything major occurring, but apart from that you can leave us and forget about us."

"What do you mean, doctor?" she asked, '"Forget you? How can I ever forget what you and Doctor Dumas have done for me? That would be impossible."

"Lucia, listen. What we have done is to help you to conceive a child, *your* child. The techniques we have used are not yet accepted by the medical profession, but we hope that one day soon they will be. In the meantime, we could not have achieved the progress we've made without the help and co-operation of you and the other lovely ladies here at the clinic. All we ask is that you give birth to a healthy child, and bring him or her up to be happy, healthy and fit in every way. We ask for no publicity. That will come later, perhaps, when Doctor Dumas has proved beyond doubt that her technique is one that will benefit thousands of women like you around the world. You have, after all, been a guinea-pig in a wholly unorthodox and unsanctioned medical trial, and publicity at this time would cause the clinic more problems than praise."

Lucia was silent for a minute. Then, she reached out and clasped Renaud's hand.

"Doctor Renaud," she spoke solemnly, "I am so very grateful to you, Doctor Dumas, and everyone here at the clinic. You have given me something that no one else in the world could have done. I will never, ever, do or say anything that may cause trouble for any of you, or the clinic. If you wish me to keep the clinic's part in my conception to myself, I can promise you that it will stay that way. Only myself and Antonio will ever know of it, unless you direct me otherwise in the future."

Renaud smiled down at Lucia, retrieved his hand from her grip, and spoke once more.

"Have no fears or worries, Lucia. Everything will be fine. You will have a beautiful child very soon, and we have a wealth of information and research data that will assist us in our future work. All we ask is that you be happy and enjoy the gift we have helped create."

"Thank you, Doctor Renaud, thank you," said Lucia, as the doctor edged towards the door.

After he'd left and she was left alone in her room once again, Lucia took a while to reflect on what the doctor had said to her. Perhaps for the first time, she realised that the project she'd been a part of was indeed highly unethical and illegal, though he'd refrained from using those words; *unorthodox and unsanctioned* had been the words he'd used, but Lucia was in no doubt as to what he'd meant. In other words, she thought that it was likely that she would be in big trouble if word of her involvement were to become public knowledge. Though her happiness at the news of her pregnancy still filled her with elation, she also knew now that the secret of her conception must remain closely guarded, unless Dumas or Renaud ever told her otherwise. Lucia vowed to herself to return home to Antonio, celebrate with him, and then try to do as Doctor Renaud had suggested, and forget about the Clinique Sobel.

All over the Blenheim Wing that day, similar conversations were held, and all of the women agreed never to divulge the involvement of the clinic in their conceptions. Though some of them were a little puzzled and perplexed by the fact that they must deny the clinic at what was probably its moment of greatest achievement, a communal fear of being exposed as part of an illegal trial, and the faintly hinted at belief that they may be subject to some form of official sanction which might affect their rights to raise their children in freedom, ensured that there was total agreement to keep the clinic's part in their conception a secret.

Thus, on what was arguably the happiest day, up until then, in the lives of those five young women, a conspiracy of silence was born that would have far reaching consequences on the lives of every one of them. But that was something that lay far in the future, and for now, happiness was the order of the day.

Chapter Seventeen

Ballater, Scotland, Christmas 1976

Angus Houston raised his glass, charged with the finest Glenfiddich malt whisky, and proposed a toast to the assembled family. "On the occasion of ma wee son's first Christmas, I shall ask ye all to drink a toast to his future happiness, aye, and to his prosperity, for 'tis sure he has a good life ahead of him. Ma friends, join wi' me in a toast, to Hamish Harry Houston!"

His father had acknowledged in the toast the name to which his son was by now universally referred, though for the toast, he used his given name first, thus keeping himself and everyone else in the room happy. Young Harry Houston simply lay on his mother's knee, dozing happily, as the family party continued around him. The child was oblivious to the raucous sounds of mirth generated by the Houston clan as they celebrated his first Christmas on earth with liberal amounts of Scotch whisky, port, sherry, fine Scottish beers and other beverages suitable for the occasion. Angus, the master butcher, had prepared a veritable family feast as was his annual custom. He'd used only the finest, prime fresh veal purchased from the not-too-far away estate of Fasque House, once the home of the Victorian prime minister William Ewart Gladstone, and now a working deer farm and visitor centre, where tourists would flock to tour the family home, with many of the rooms open to public view.

Young Harry Houston's first Christmas was filled with laughter and gaiety, the child surrounded by happy, proud parents and loving aunts and uncles, cousins and grandparents. It was the first of many spent in the family home, and, as a carpet of crisp, white frost gave the false impression of a traditional white Christmas to the land around the Houston home, the trees bending their branches in the cold, damp air, there was probably not a happier family in the whole of Scotland during that year's festive season.

Turin, Christmas 1976

Lucia Cannavaro was enjoying her pregnancy. She was four months away from giving birth to her very own baby, and she couldn't have been happier. Her mother-in-law had invited her and Antonio to visit her for the holiday, but Lucia had pleaded with Antonio until he'd agreed that they would spend Christmas together in their tiny apartment. Lucia had wanted to cook a traditional Christmas meal for the two of them to enjoy in the peace and quiet of their own home, as she knew that this time the following year they would have the baby to occupy them. It would be more intimate and romantic, she'd told Antonio, to spend this special time together, just the two of them, and her husband had agreed.

Christmas 1976, various locations

In New York, London, Zurich, and Dublin, there were other families with good reason to celebrate the festive season with a sense of optimism and joy. The pregnancies of Tilly Garrelli, Elizabeth Hammond, Katerina Todt, and Theresa Dunne were all proceeding exactly as they should. There had been no problems or complications to contend with for any of the women, all of whom were considered by their doctors to be in the most remarkable health. Together with their respective husbands they, like Lucia Cannavaro, were all looking forward with eager and joyous anticipation for the day in just a few short months when they would bring their babies into the world and their dreams of motherhood would be finally fulfilled. Since the day they had left the Clinique Sobel they had heard nothing from either Doctor Renaud or Doctor Dumas, as they'd expected, but, just two days before Christmas, each family had received a small, handwritten Christmas card with a Belgian postmark. Inside the card was written in the unmistakeable hand of Doctor Alexander Renaud, which they all recognised from their time at the clinic, "A Christmas wish for you, be safe and well, may your future be all you hope for. A.R." They all thought it typical of the kind and caring Doctor Renaud that he would take the time to send them his good wishes, unofficially of course. They neither received nor expected any similar gesture from Doctor Margherita Dumas. For all of the women who had recently occupied the rooms of the Blenheim Wing at the Clinique Sobel, it was a happy and dream-filled Christmas. They knew that their dreams were about to come true; nothing else could intrude on those thoughts.

Ostend, Belgium, Christmas 1976

The woman sat quietly sipping from a glass of chardonnay as she watched the two boys. There in the specially adapted windowless playroom, the two children sat on the cushions on the floor watching the flickering images on the television screen in front of them. The TV had been the latest addition to the room's equipment, though viewing was strictly rationed and carefully selected. Now, on Christmas day, the two boys were being fed a visual diet of images from the Vietnam War, of death and human destruction, of blood and bodies and carnage.

There were no decorations in the room, no presents, no songs of joy, and no Christmas carols. For the two little boys in that sealed environment there was no such event as Christmas. It was unknown to them; as unknown as it would have been to the crew of an alien space craft had it landed on earth at that moment.

The sound of gunfire and explosions filled the room. The boys watched, transfixed, as images of helicopter gunships sprayed hot metal death into the ground below and large high-flying aircraft sent plumes of deforesting chemicals sweeping to the earth, destroying the green forest. They saw the screaming jets as they unleashed their loads of napalm-infused bombs on villages containing women, children and just perhaps, the enemy. There were pictures of the armies of both sides, young men old before their time, covered in blood and filth, faces devoid of feeling and understanding.

The two little boys waited until the video tape had finished, and then they asked if they could watch it again.

Chapter Eighteen

Ballater, Scotland, March 1977

Ten-month-old Harry Houston was growing up fast. The youngster had taken his first tentative steps a couple of weeks before his tenth month, and had spoken his first word, 'Dada,' mere days later. His mother was fiercely proud of her little son, and young Harry was the star attraction at the many family get-togethers organised in the Houston home. As for Angus, the development of the off-shore oil industry was doing wonders for Scotland's local economy and for Aberdeen in particular. The port of that city had become the home base for much of the service industry that had sprung up to support the vast oil rigs which had taken root in the North Sea off the coast of North-East Scotland. As for the surrounding area, the presence of so many oil industry workers had led to a call for a vast building programme. Those workers needed homes for their families within reach of the port from which they would sail, or within distance of the airport from which fleets of helicopters ferried the rig workers back and forth as they alternated between home and work, usually on a three-week on, three-week off cycle.

All of this was good news for Angus Houston, as with the influx of newcomers to the area, his business grew and his profits increased in tandem with the population expansion. Although Ballater was some distance from the city, this was no deterrent to the oil workers, many of whom wanted to put some miles between themselves and their work when at home, and the sheer beauty of the village, and its neighbours Aboyne and Banchory, proved irresistible to many of those involved in the industry.

As spring approached, the long-time owner of the store next to the butcher shop died. Angus made an offer to buy it, and, his offer accepted by the man's heirs, he doubled the size of his by now very well known shop and further expanded his bourgeoning business. Angus Houston worked tirelessly, his one goal being to build a foundation for his family's long-term prosperity and particularly to produce a profitable legacy to leave to his young son Harry when the time came.

New York, 15th March 1977

Just as many women had done before her, as the woman had done almost three years before, Tilly Garrelli screamed, but her scream was one of joy, of triumph, as her new born baby son made his grand entrance into the world. Vincent was with her throughout the birth, holding her hand and passing her the mask that dispensed the gas and oxygen mix to help with the pain of her contractions whenever she needed it. Peter Garrelli was born at ten-thirty in the morning, and his parents felt themselves blessed by God and as happy as a man and woman could possibly be.

London, the same day.

The birth of John Hammond was just as momentous a moment for his parents as Peter Garrelli's was for his. The joy and celebration that greeted their infant son simply shone on the proud faces of Elizabeth and Michael Hammond. Even the recent death of Michael's mother in a tragic road accident some weeks earlier couldn't detract from the overwhelming sense of happiness that pervaded the hospital's delivery room as Elizabeth lay relaxing after the birth, cradling her new born son on her chest, her husband gazing in adoration at his family from the chair beside the bed.

Various locations, the same day

The Garrellis and the Hammonds would perhaps have been surprised to learn of the almost simultaneous births of each other's baby boys that day. They would have been totally astounded had they known that Lucia Cannavaro in Turin, Theresa Dunne in Dublin, and Katerina Todt in Zurich had all given birth to their miracle babies at virtually the same time. The scenes of happiness and celebration that had marked the births of little Peter and John were reflected in hospitals around Europe as all the women from the Blenheim Wing at the Clinique Sobel delivered their children on the same date. Had they all known of the momentous and highly improbable set of circumstances surrounding the births of their children, the women might have paused to wonder how such a thing could have happened. Could coincidence have stretched quite that far?

In Turin, Lucia Cannavaro voiced perhaps just one of many similar questions that day when she said to her husband some hours after the birth of her son Angelo, "Antonio, after having done so much for us, is it not a little strange that the clinic did not even want us to let them know when our baby was born? Surely the birth is the proof they need of the reliability of Doctor Dumas's procedures?

"Maybe they have ways of finding these things out for themselves, Lucia. If we contacted them it would be going against everything they asked you to adhere to when you left the clinic, and could cause trouble for the doctor. We must try to remember that. Yet I'm sure they will know somehow that we have our baby boy. Perhaps someone here in the hospital is in contact with them, or even Doctor Menotti."

Doctor Menotti was their own physician, and it had been he who had conducted the original tests on Lucia on behalf of the clinic. He'd attended Lucia throughout her pregnancy, though he'd made no further reference to the clinic, not even once.

"Hmm, maybe," said Lucia, dreamily, as she drifted off into a deep sleep, tired from the exertions of giving birth to her beautiful son. The last thing she thought of before sleep took her was that her son had been born on the Ides of March, the date made famous in history as the day of the assassination of Julius Caesar, and she thought that perhaps her son may one day be a new leader of men, like the great Caesar of history.

None of the women had kept in touch with each other after leaving the clinic. The rules governing the use of first names only had ensured that no full names had been exchanged, no addresses swapped, and therefore no communication between the women had been possible. If there had been, perhaps a note of caution, a hint of something being not quite as it should have been about their children's births, might have crept into the minds of those ecstatic new mothers. Apart from the timing, all five babies were boys, all weighed the same at birth, and all had a covering of thick dark hair on their heads. Had the parents been able to compare them, they would have been more than a little astounded at the almost unbelievable similarities between their children.

As it was, unbounded joy was the overpowering emotion that day in so many delivery rooms and maternity wards. There were tears of joy, hugs and kisses between adoring parents, congratulations poured in to the various couples from doctors, nurses, friends and family. Nothing could or would be allowed to spoil the day when the babies of the Blenheim Wing gave voice to their first cries, and five new lives began.

Chapter Nineteen

Ostend, Belgium, March 1977

The man and the woman sat at either end of the large, comfortable sofa, the two boys, Arturo and Alexei, between them. They were watching the television, which was reporting the news. The picture showed a scene of flaming conflagration as the reporter stated that earlier that day fire had destroyed the Clinique Sobel, a fertility clinic on the outskirts of Brussels. The clinic had been operated by Doctor Alexander Renaud under the overall direction of Doctor Margherita Dumas, one of the world's most prominent pioneers in the field of human infertility. The reporter went on to state that there had been no casualties, all the staff and patients having been evacuated at the first signs of fire having broken out. Neither Doctor Renaud nor Doctor Dumas had been available for comment at the time of the report being made, but a spokesman for the clinic had expressed their sadness that so much important work and research had gone up in smoke, possibly never to be repeated in the future. They were, however, happy that no-one had been hurt in the blaze, while of course saddened that the clinic had been gutted and was obviously totally beyond any hope of economic repair.

"Tragic," said the woman.

"Absolutely," said the man.

"Fire burns," said Arturo.

"Very hot," continued Alexei.

"Fire kills," came from Arturo.

"Pretty fire," this from Alexei.

"Now boys, that's enough," commanded the woman.

"They're developing a cruel streak for two so young," the man said softly to the woman.

"They're becoming realists, that's all," was her reply. "They will gradually become desensitised to these things, they will be devoid of the stupid sentimentality that pervades the minds of the woolly-headed liberals that want to shape our modern society. These boys will know the reality of the world, its pain, its deceit, its fickleness, and one day, they will make a difference. Now, let's be quiet everyone, and watch the fire, eh?"

The four of them fell silent, as the flames on the television news report seemed to reach higher into the sky, reaching for the clouds, as the Clinique Sobel's roof collapsed in on itself. The last pictures shown in the news report were of the Blenheim Wing as its walls came crashing down. Then the picture changed as another, less important story took the place of the Brussels fire.

The boys were bored, and got up from the sofa. They made their way to the cushions in the corner, curled up together, and were asleep in a matter of seconds.

The man and the woman left the room through the locked door to the office and left the boys to sleep, lulled by the reassuring sound of the incessant, ever present air conditioning.

Chapter Twenty

Margherita Dumas sat opposite Alexander Renaud at one of the best tables in the restaurant. Located on Grand Place in Brussels, the Maison du Cygne was one of her favourite haunts, and served some of the best food in the city. It had been a month since the fire had destroyed the Clinique Sobel, and the fire brigade inquiry into the cause had finally concluded that the fire had started accidentally, when a burner in one of the laboratories had been inadvertently left on, close to a window that had been left open for ventilation. A gust of wind had probably blown the burner over, and the flame had ignited certain flammable chemicals in a nearby Petri dish which had formed part of an earlier experiment in the lab. It had perhaps resulted from a case of sloppy technical procedure by someone in the lab, but that was the extent of the brigade's investigating officer's criticism.

"So, my friend, what do we do now that our clinic is no more?" asked Dumas of her dinner companion.

"I think you know very well what happens next, my good doctor, don't you?" replied Renaud.

Margherita Dumas smiled at Renaud, taking a moment to savour the flavour of the superb fresh mussels on her plate. "Our research at the Clinique Sobel is ended, as we knew it would be when the children were born. Our friends around the world have kept us informed of each and every birth without ever knowing who we are. You hired them anonymously and paid them well to send information to the post-restante address when the babies arrived. We know that they were all born exactly according to plan, on time, and in good health. We cannot be traced either to the fire, or to the children. All the mothers will keep silent about our involvement. I think we made it clear to them all that they might be at risk of losing their babies if they talked of their treatment at the clinic. We can watch them from afar, there are always those who will be our eyes and ears if the price is right, but, I warn you, Renaud, change them frequently, these spies you employ. Don't take the chance that one of them might learn too much and start to add things together. If that were ever to happen, we would have to resort to, shall I say, sterner measures to ensure their continued silence."

"Don't worry, doctor. Our secret is safe, and will remain so."

"I hope so, Renaud, for both our sakes, I hope so."

"I'm just amazed at how easily the women accepted our instructions not to ever mention the clinic," said Renaud.

"Ah, but we chose our guinea pigs wisely, my friend did we not? They were all desperate for a child, from small poorish families, and they would have agreed to anything as long as we gave them what they wanted. For them, a baby was worth more than any financial fortune in the world. We gave them their dream. They will never let us down."

"Will they ever learn the truth, do you think?" asked Renaud.

"Why should they?" replied Dumas. "They all believe that their children are the result of implanting their own husband's sperm into their eggs. We were careful in selecting only those women whose husbands fit the necessary physical characteristics that we needed in order to carry out the project. No, Alexander, my dear friend, they will never know."

Dumas usually only referred to Renaud by his first name when she was relaxed, as she was now becoming. Perhaps it was the food, or the wine, or a little of both, but she felt as though a great weight had been lifted from her ever since the clinic had been reduced to a smouldering pile of ashes. The truth of what they'd done was contained in files that had been obliterated by the fire. There was a second set of those files, but they were held somewhere so secure, so safe, that she had no fears of them ever being discovered, and in that set, all the participants were identified solely by code numbers. There were no names written down at all, not even first names.

Renaud and Dumas continued their meal, and the two of them relaxed even further, to the extent that they began not to talk of medical matters at all, but of things closer to home. That was very unusual between the two of them, for they normally maintained a close but wholly professional relationship. As they sipped coffee and ate a selection of small chocolate mints provided by the waiter, Renaud suddenly dropped his bombshell for the evening.

"I'm getting married," he announced, softly, but with a hard edge to his voice.

"You're what?" Dumas snapped, almost choking on a mint.

"I'm getting married," he repeated.

"But, how can you? What about our work? When did you meet her? Who is she? How long has this been going on?"

For one normally so calm, Margherita Dumas was giving a good impression of someone on the verge of losing her self control. What she'd just heard had taken the wind out of her sails. She felt betrayed and terribly let down by the man sitting at the other side of the table.

"Our work will go on," he replied, still in that soft and reassuring voice that so beguiled the women he met every day of his life. "There is no reason why we cannot continue to work together. Marlette is quite conversant with my medical work, in the loosest sense, of course. She knows I am involved with certain fields of research, and that I work with you. She admires you greatly, I may add. Marlette and I met a year ago. We are very much in love, and the wedding will take place in two months time. I hope, Doctor Dumas, that you will do me the honour of attending the service."

Though the news had come as a surprise to her, Dumas realised that it should not have. Alexander Renaud was, after all, an extremely handsome man. It would have been only a matter of time before some woman had come along and found the key to his heart, and this Marlette, whoever she was, had obviously done just that. The doctor knew just what she must do.

"Well, my friend. I'm flabbergasted, I must admit. You have given me a hell of a surprise, but, after all, what can I say? I must congratulate you, both of you, and also chide you, Alexander, for not mentioning this lady to me before. Did you think I would try to come between the two of you? Was that it? Don't worry, I'm happy for you, really I am. My, but good Doctor Renaud, you are becoming an expert at keeping secrets, aren't you?" she asked with a conspiratorial wink of the eye. "Have no fear, I will be there for you on the day. I shall happily dance at your wedding."

With that, Dumas raised her glass high, and, in a voice loud enough so that all the other customers in the restaurant could clearly hear her, she said, "To you and your wife to be. I wish you long life and happiness together, my *very, very* good friend and colleague."

Renaud accepted the toast, they touched glasses in order to seal the toast, and the two of them spent a convivial half hour during which he regaled Dumas with the tale of how he and Marlette had found love with each other. He explained that he hadn't told Dumas about the love affair between them as he did not want to deflect either of them from their important work, and again reassured her that his marriage need not affect their work together in any way at all.

As they parted with great bonhomie on the steps of the restaurant that night, she watched his taxi disappear down the street as she waited for her own prearranged cab to arrive. Margherita Dumas had already decided that Renaud was no longer to be trusted, and that she would find a way to exclude him from any future plans she may develop. She would have to find a way to achieve that goal without alienating him too far, for Alexander Renaud knew too much!

Chapter Twenty-One

Brussels, June 1977

The wedding had been a quiet affair, not at all what Margherita Dumas had expected. She'd thought that Renaud would have wanted to make a grand gesture on the day he sealed his love for his bride Marlette. As it was, the guest list had been kept to a minimum, just a few close friends and family, and the service had taken place in a quiet secluded church on the outskirts of town, close to where Marlette had lived with her parents.

She'd behaved like the perfect friend and colleague towards Renaud all day, and then, shortly before the couple had departed from the reception at a small hotel to begin the journey to the airport to catch their honeymoon flight, she cornered the groom in a quiet corner of the room. "Alexander, I don't want to spoil your day, but I must speak with you."

"What is it Margherita? Can't it wait until after I return from my honeymoon?"

"I'm sorry, my friend, no it can't. I must find a new outlet for my research. I am going to fund a new facility, but it will not be in Belgium. It will take some time to find a location and establish it, but when I do, I will not be spending as much time here as I do now. We will of course continue to work together on the Genesis Project, which is of vital importance, but I wanted you to know that things will be different when you return."

Renaud smiled, as if he'd been expecting something like this.

"Margherita, don't worry. I will be fine. I know you need a new challenge, and it would not really be advisable to set up another clinic in Belgium so soon after the Sobel."

"Not a clinic, Alexander, a pure research facility."

"Yes, as you say, but how will we continue with Genesis if you are not even in the country?"

"I will be a figurehead for the new facility. There will be staff to take care of the day-to-day running of the establishment. I will be here often enough to take care of things, and together we will oversee the project until the subjects are ready for independence. In the meantime, I will set up a new Genesis house in the new location so that we may travel between the two."

"I see," said Renaud. "And how will we explain…?

"Leave that to me. I will take care of everything," she responded.

Alexander and Marlette Renaud left for their honeymoon in Hawaii a little while later. Margherita Dumas joined the happy throng of family and friendly well-wishers who waved their cab off as it left to deliver them to the airport.

She later reflected that it had been easier than she could have hoped for to give Renaud the news. She thought he might have been angry that she wasn't going to rebuild in Belgium and continue their close association, but then, she'd never been in love and didn't realise that Renaud now had more to concentrate on than the problems of other women's infertility, or indeed perhaps, and slightly more worrying, the Genesis Project. Renaud would need watching, and closely.

Chapter Twenty-Two

Ostend, June 1977

The woman watched silently as the two boys watched yet more of their diet of televised images of war, of man's inhumanity to man, scenes of the holocaust, and she smiled to herself. The little boys had become almost totally desensitized to the sight and sound of human suffering. They had come to see death as an integral part of life, and the word, and the event itself, held no fear for them. That was as she wanted it.

Intellectually, they were developing just as she had predicted they would. They had the quickness of mind, the dexterity of hand, and the analytical skills typified by the man whose genes had joined with hers to create the boys. They had seen themselves as the perfect progenitors, the ideal standard on which future generations should be built. Now, all they had to do was prove it.

Others might think that they could modify the human model to satisfy the needs of the parent, or of society, and many had tried, but she knew without a doubt that where the others had failed, and would continue to fail, she had succeeded. Her boys would prove her right, of that she was sure.

Even Hitler had failed. His attempt to create a master race of pure Aryan stock had resulted in total and unmitigated disaster. The Americans, the Russians, the British, even others here in Belgium thought they could beat her to the secret, but they wouldn't, they couldn't, because she'd already unlocked that secret, and there it was, sitting on the floor, watching scenes of horror from around the world, the sound turned up loud to accentuate the devastation that was being portrayed.

The two boys looked up at her and smiled, and their smiles were a mixture of the innocence of infancy and the knowledge brought about by their constant exposure to the dark side of man. Soon, she thought, they would be ready for the next step in their education. But for now, culture could wait. Education was finding a new level in that air-conditioned room, where the sun never shone, and the birds didn't sing.

She smiled back at the boys, who ran to the sofa and took up positions either side of her. They sat quietly until she ordered them to turn off the TV, and Arturo obeyed instantly.

"Sleep," she ordered, and the two little boys ran to the pile of waiting cushions, curled up together like young wolves nestling together for warmth, and in seconds they were asleep.

The woman waited a minute, and then approached the sleeping boys with two syringes she'd kept hidden in her jacket pocket. The injections she administered as they slept would ensure they wouldn't wake for some time and would give her plenty of time to do what she had to before returning to the windowless room once more.

In two minutes she was gone, and the boys slept, and dreamed, and the imagery of their dreams was indescribable.

Part II

THE PASSAGE OF TIME

Chapter Twenty-Three

Ostend, Belgium, Spring 1989

The sound of the piano concerto filled the room, and the woman closed her eyes and allowed the music to enter into her mind, her soul. The boy, a young man now, was incredibly handsome, and his hands moved with the practised skill of a concert pianist as they danced across the keys, almost in a blur. At his side his brother stood, violin in hand, ready to reinforce the performance. As his hand moved to draw the bow across the strings of the instrument and the two of them began to play together, the woman was enraptured by what she heard.

Arturo and Alexei were fifteen years old, though the casual observer would have taken them for twenty at least. They were tall, well-muscled, and athletically built, and the woman considered that the time she'd invested in them, in their unusual education, had all been worthwhile. They were intelligent, well schooled in all manner of educational core subjects, and fluent in five languages. They had the charm and wit of adults twice their age, and were musically talented, as was evidenced by their current performance.

To that casual onlooker, they would have appeared to be quite the child prodigies, and indeed, they were most certainly educated to a standard far beyond that expected of an average fifteen-year-old. What that observer might have found however, had they taken the time to delve a little further, would have been two young men who displayed an almost amoral attitude to their fellow human beings. Here were two young men who saw no wrong in the use of murder or extortion in order to achieve an objective, and who valued human life cheaply, not as a thing to be cherished, but as a commodity to be exploited for whatever use could be made of it. Their strange upbringing had made them incapable of displaying any feeling toward their fellows. The only spark of love within them was reserved for the woman who sat watching them, and for the man who they knew as Papa. They looked very much like him in fact–uncannily so, to tell the truth.

Aboyne Academy, Aboyne, Scotland, May, 1989

Young Harry Houston hated parents' evenings. In particular he had a major dislike of the fact that he had to sit between his mother and father, in front of teachers who talked about him as if he wasn't there, like he was invisible to them. Right now they were doing just that, his mother and father deep in conversation with Mr. McAdam, the careers master. Harry had just passed his thirteenth birthday and was still some years away from leaving school, yet the headmaster encouraged all the children of Harry's age and above to have regular meetings with the careers master, to discuss their future career paths. Harry had been dreading this night, as he knew that Mr. McAdam was about to blow his big secret, and his father wouldn't be pleased, of that he was sure.

"He *what?*" blasted Houston senior, so loud that every head in the room turned in his direction. "A police officer? You say he wants to be a police officer? This boy hasnae' a hope in hell of that, let me be telling ye. He's to follow me into the business, that's what he's goin' to do."

That was it, thought Harry, the secret was out.

Mr. McAdam spoke quietly and soothingly to Angus Houston in an attempt to calm the red-faced butcher down.

"Mr. Houston, please listen. At the moment Harry is too young to make any hard and fast decisions about his future. We merely encourage the children here at school to look at options for the future, and we provide them with all the information they need to make informed opinions about what they may want to do when they eventually leave school. I have to say that from the day he started here, Harry has always expressed a desire to join the police force when he grows up and leaves home."

McAdam's last sentence had been a second bombshell to Harry's father, whose red face now assumed an even darker shade of that colour as he responded loudly, "Grows up and leaves home now is it? Just what are ye doing to the children at this school, may I ask, encouraging them to take on careers against the wishes of their families, and wanting them to leave their homes and go gallivanting around the country pursuing some stupid childish pipedream? Ma son is goin' to be a butcher I tell you, did you hear me? *A butcher!*"

"You have another son, Mr. Houston. Have you ever thought that Duncan might want to take over the business from you one day?"

"Duncan? Why, he's no more than a bairn, and Harry's the eldest. It's his place to take over when I retire."

"Mr. Houston, I can only ask that you go home and talk to your children. Find out how they feel about things. It's their lives we're talking about after all. We can't always live our dreams through our children, as much as we may want to. Talk to the boys, Mr. Houston, please."

So it was that Angus Houston was faced with the very real possibility that his eldest son wanted no part in the business that he, Angus, had spent a lifetime building.

Sitting at home later that night, his second son Duncan, then just ten years old, told his parents that he wanted to be a butcher like his father when he grew up. Angus Houston smiled, but growled through his teeth when Harry reiterated his desire to become a police officer. It was Harry's mother who eventually took the heat out of the situation when she simply said, "Well, Angus, I think it will be very nice to have a policeman in the family. Harry will look *wonderful* in a uniform, and the shop will be just as well looked after by Duncan when the time comes, and, be honest, you'll be as proud as I will to see your son striding down the street enforcing the law of the land."

Angus Houston was a stubborn and a proud man, but he knew when to admit defeat. With Margaret on Harry's side, he was never going to win, and he knew that it wouldn't be right to force the boy into a career he didn't have the heart for. He remembered thinking to himself that he wished he hadn't bought that cheap plastic policeman's helmet from a market stall in Aberdeen all those Christmasses ago. Harry had placed it on his head, and played with it for far longer than any of his more expensive presents. In fact he'd played with it for years, and the damned thing was still tucked away in the corner of the boy's wardrobe in his bedroom. Angus decided there and then that he had indeed been the architect of his own downfall on this occasion, and the gruff and dour butcher smiled and gave in gracefully, not for the first time in his life, for underneath that tough exterior there beat a heart of gold, belonging to a man who idolised his wife and children, and who would do anything to see them happy. He just didn't always show it, that was all.

"Right, well then," he said, "Constable Houston it shall be then, but you mind my words young Harry. Ye'll carry on working in the shop on Saturdays until ye leave that school of yours, you just think on, now."

Harry and his mother smiled back at Angus, who put his arm around his eldest son, and Harry looked up at his father in gratitude "Aye, thank you, father, I'll not let you down."

At that point, young Harry's career path was set, and unknown to the boy, he had just taken the first step down the road that would lead him to one of the most bizarre and unusual cases in criminal history, though for now that was still a long way away. Harry's appointment with fate had been made; he just didn't know it yet.

Chapter Twenty-Four

Turin, Christmas 1989

The news programmes on the television for the last few days had been filled with stories of the American invasion of Panama, U.S. troops being deployed to capture General Manuel Noriega, a successful mission that would eventually see the Panamanian drug lord sentenced to 40 years imprisonment. In Europe, Christmas day itself was marked by the execution, in Rumania, of deposed Communist hard-line president Nikolae Ceauşesccu and his wife Elena following the popular uprising that had overthrown his government.

In the tiny apartment home of the Cannavaros in the centre of the city of Turin, however, these and other world events were reduced to triviality by the happy little family that sat around the glittering lights of the cheap but brightly lit Christmas tree which now stood centre-stage in the living room. Lucia and Antonio Cannavaro watched their twelve-year-old son Angelo as he played happily with the few toys and games they'd managed to afford in order to give their son a happy Christmas. Times were still hard for the Cannavaros, but, as they did every year, they managed to put their financial worries aside for a few weeks to ensure that their son, who they adored beyond belief, would have the Christmas he deserved.

As Angelo Cannavaro played with his toys and laughed and giggled at the antics of his parents who joined in with his enjoyment, similar scenes were being played out in New York, London, Dublin, and Zurich, as the other children of the Blenheim Wing enjoyed Christmas with their parents. For some, it would be the last happy one for a while.

Ostend, Belgium, Christmas 1989

The woman sat watching Arturo and Alexei as they in turn sat watching the video tape she'd inserted into the VCR. The two boys were enthralled by the scenes of mayhem and death that played across the TV screen. They'd seen this tape many times before, but never ceased to be entertained by the visions of the slaughtering of the innocents undertaken by the Chinese Army earlier that year following the student protests in Tiananmen Square.

Papa would not be with them again for Christmas. Though they saw him from time to time, Mama had told them a long time ago that Papa had other things to do with his life, he couldn't stay with them all the time anymore, and they had accepted the news matter-of-factly. The woman was aware, though, that she had said just enough over the years to ensure that the boys would always follow her instructions. Papa was a secondary figure in their lives, and always would be.

She left the boys happily watching the scenes of slaughter on the television and returned through the connecting door to the office. Looking up from time to time to observe the boys on the camera over her head, she took a few minutes to go through some of the papers on the desk. Finding an envelope with the easily recognisable handwriting of the man on it, she opened it to find two Christmas cards inside. One was for her, which she read, and then placed in her handbag; it could go on her mantelpiece later. The other was addressed to Arturo and Alexei, and signed "From Papa." With a twisted smile playing across her face, the woman threw it in the waste paper bin.

Chapter Twenty-Five

In the six months after Christmas, a series of strange and tragic events began to overtake the families of the children of the Blenheim Wing. Less than a month into the New Year, Antonio Cannavaro was struck by a hit-and run driver as he walked home from work one night, just after dark. The only witness to the accident, a less than reliable drunk who was on his way home from a bar and who saw the whole thing from the comfort of the kerb he'd sat down upon to rest his unresponsive legs, reported to the police that Antonio had been crossing the road when the car seemed to appear from nowhere and accelerate straight at the poor man. The collision between car and man had been so violent that Antonio's body had been hurled completely over the car's roof, and he'd landed with a sickening thud on his head, as the car sped off without stopping. The drunk couldn't be sure, but he thought that the driver, who was wearing a hat, could have been a woman. He hadn't taken the registration number of the car, he was too shocked by what he'd witnessed, drunk or not. Antonio Cannavaro was dead long before the ambulance and the police arrived on the scene.

In February, Vincent Garrelli fell from the platform of a subway station, straight under the wheels of the subway train that was arriving at the station at that moment. The platform had been crowded, with the usual rush hour crowds jostling and jockeying for position as they waited for their train. Even so, there were one or two of the crowd who swore to the police that they saw a woman dressed all in black, with a hooded jacket pulled over her head, standing right behind Vincent just before he fell. The general consensus among those witnesses was that the unknown woman had pushed Vincent Garrelli, who was killed instantly as the wheels of the train crushed his skull like a vice squashing a melon. The subsequent police investigation found no evidence of foul play. There was nothing to corroborate the witness' theories of the woman in black.

Two weeks after the death of Vincent Garrelli, Elizabeth Hammond became the third of the Sobel women to be widowed. Her husband Michael appeared to have been the victim of a freak accident at the airport where he'd worked for over twenty years. Whist unloading freight from a 747 that had recently arrived from Athens, Michael had been killed when a large packing case slipped from a fork lift truck and fell directly onto his head, causing instantaneous death. The load had been secured incorrectly, and the webbing straps that should have held it in place even though it was unbalanced on the palette had been weakened through constant use and had snapped as the weight of the case veered wildly off centre. The British airport police who investigated the incident at one time held a theory that the webbing straps might have been deliberately weakened by having a sharp object systematically rubbed along the surface over a period of time, ensuring that a sudden heavy weight pulling against them would cause them to snap, but they had no proof that that had been the case, and there appeared to be no motive for anyone to want to kill an inoffensive baggage handler. The strange thing about the case as far as the police were concerned was that the packing case fell just as Michael marshalled the truck into place, as it was directly in front of him, and the case would therefore have fallen directly onto him as the truck braked, and if it had been premeditated, how could the killer have known exactly how much to weaken the straps to make it fall at that moment?

The biggest discrepancy came from one witness, a member of the baggage handling crew, who told the police that certain last minute adjustments to the load were made by a woman handler before it left from the loading area under the aircraft's hold. No-one else saw the woman, and the airport personnel records showed that no female handlers were on duty in that area, so the witness was eventually regarded as having been mistaken. One of the police officers involved in the investigation thought that there was more to the incident than was being discovered, but, as a coroner's court recorded a verdict of accidental death, there was nothing he could do to pursue the case.

If the women who had given birth to those beautiful children on the Ides of March in 1977 had been able to keep in touch, it would have been a sure bet that Theresa Dunne and Katerina Todt would have been extremely disturbed about the fate of the three men who had been married to Lucia Cannavaro, Elizabeth Hammond, and Tilly Garrelli. As it was, they had no idea of the events that had taken place around the world, so were blissfully ignorant of any possible danger to their own spouses, and, after all, the authorities had listed all three deaths as accidental, so what was there to fear?

The next to suffer the vagaries of fate, as it seemed, was poor Katerina Todt. Her husband, Wilhelm, had been working late, and was on his way home, when he was approached by a woman he'd never met before. She asked him for directions to the City Bank Corporation's headquarters, and Wilhelm told her it was just across the bridge they were approaching. He offered to show her the way. As they crossed the bridge, the woman suddenly screamed and pointed at something in the river below. As he peered over the wall of the bridge, she grabbed him by the feet and in one sudden and swift movement catapulted him forward and downwards into the swirling black water forty feet below the bridge. He hit the water and was gone in seconds. Wilhelm Todt had never learned to swim and his body was found the next morning on the bank of the river, with no signs of foul play evident. There had been no witnesses to his death, and it was assumed he'd fallen whilst looking over the parapet of the bridge, or even worse, had committed suicide, which Katerina resolutely refused to believe. She told the investigators that they were a happy couple with a wonderful son, and that there was no reason on earth why Wilhelm would have wanted to take his own life. Almost inevitably his death was recorded as accidental.

On the first day of May, as Mayday celebrations took place around the world, Patrick Dunne set sail in his fishing coble early in the morning. He intended to fish for lobster as usual, and was a mere mile from shore when a sudden explosion ripped through the boat. The engine had been playing up and he'd bent over the troublesome machine to try to correct the problem, which he'd thought was probably caused by a fault in the fuel pump. As he'd lifted the cowling that covered the small engine, the last thing he saw was a blinding flash as the explosion threw him backwards across the deck, his face a mass of flames, his hands clawing at his searing flesh. The flames quickly spread to the rest of his body, and Patrick Dunne died as his body twisted in one last agonising attempt to escape the flames that consumed him and fell over the low gunwale of his boat into the depths of the ocean. The flames that had claimed Patrick had spread to the boat, which followed its owner to the bottom of the sea in a very short time. Unfortunately, no-one on shore or at sea had witnessed the tragedy, and although Theresa reported her husband missing when he failed to return home that night, it was three weeks before his body was washed up on shore, by which time there was little left even to confirm his identity, let alone determine the cause of death. Only an eventual check of dental records proved the identity of the body. The remains of his boat were never found; they reside somewhere under the rolling waves of the Irish Sea, all evidence of his demise long since erased.

The whole of Patrick's local community attended his funeral; such was the shock at his sudden and untimely death. There was much sadness and sympathy for his poor wife Theresa and her young son, Patrick junior. The death of Theresa's husband had of course been recorded as a tragic accident.

Between January and May of the year nineteen ninety, every one of the women who had given birth after receiving treatment in the Blenheim Wing of the Clinique Sobel in nineteen seventy-six had become a widow. No one knew of or could possibly suspect any connection between the deaths of men who lived as far apart from each other as New York and Turin, Dublin and Zurich, for there was nothing recorded anywhere that would connect those men's lives together. That, of course, was just the way it was supposed to be.

Chapter Twenty-Six

The Strada Institute, Zurich, July 1994

"So, Margherita, all goes well with you, I see. This institute has become a truly wondrous place, a beacon for the research you always wanted to do. People from around the world respect and honour you for the work you are doing here. You are to be congratulated."

Margherita Dumas nodded in appreciation. It had been some time since she'd seen Renaud in person, though they kept in regular contact by telephone. The two doctors were still bound by the ties of years ago, and though Dumas would have preferred it if she had never seen Renaud again, she knew it was necessary that they meet from time to time. Indeed, it was she who had asked him to attend this meeting at her pristine research facility on the outskirts of the beautiful city of Zurich.

Renaud continued, "What a long way you've come since those days at the Sobel, eh? From a humble specialist in human embryology and fertilisation to one of the world's leading researchers in the field of cloning. My, you have gone up in the world!"

There was a degree of irony in Renaud's voice that wasn't lost on Dumas. "Really, Alexander. If I didn't know you better, I'd think there was a hint of jealousy in your voice."

"Nothing of the sort, Margherita, nothing of the sort. I merely point out that those who parade your name from the rooftops might think a little differently if they knew what you and I had done all those years ago, that's all. What we did *was* fundamentally wrong, you do know that, don't you?"

"Wrong? How can you say it was wrong? What we did was to achieve nothing short of a miracle! We pushed the boundaries of medical science and technology to their absolute limits and beyond, and we succeeded where no-one else would even have tried."

"Yes, we did, but we can never tell anyone, can we?"

"We don't need to, can't you see that? What we learned has been put to good use, and I don't see you returning the cheques I regularly deposit in your bank account as your share of that project, now do I?"

Renaud fell silent.

"It is of the Genesis Project that I wish to speak today," she continued. "There may be a small problem with the original experimental subjects."

"Those 'experimental subjects' are living beings. They have names; you named them, for God's sake. We shared their upbringing until you cut me off from them. I hardly see them at all now, apart from when you deem it suitable for me to pay a visit, or when you bring them back to Belgium on your trips home."

"Yes, they have names, of course they do. So do pet dogs, cats, and hamsters. We couldn't bring them up referring to them by their experimental reference numbers, could we? It doesn't change the fact that that's what they are. An experiment, a long and time-consuming one, yes, but an experiment nonetheless."

"God, but you sound heartless sometimes, do you know that? Don't you have any feelings for them at all? They came from your own womb!"

"Oh, come now, Renaud; don't go getting sentimental on me. You knew what we were doing when we started. Don't pretend you didn't."

"Get to the point. What's this 'problem' with the boys you talked about?"

"It's the irradiated cells. They're causing some unforeseen medical complications in the boys."

"What sort of complications?" asked Renaud with a look of deep concern suddenly appearing on his face.

"Well," said Dumas, "For one thing, their metabolic rate is increasing, slowly and almost imperceptibly, but it's increasing, and there's no medical reason why it should. Also, certain of their internal organs are showing signs of premature degeneration. It's as if the irradiated cells we added to the process have begun some sort of breakdown process. I don't know yet if it's a permanent condition or if I can somehow reverse it. I need your help. You must come and see them, give me your opinion."

"What about a hospital?" asked Renaud.

"You fool!" snapped Dumas. "How can I take them to a hospital? They'd ask too many questions, and if the truth were to come out, we'd both end up behind bars for a very long time. You should know that."

Renaud responded after a moment's thought. "I think what you're saying is that the irradiated material we included in their make-up has started some sort of internal chain reaction, and you don't know how to stop it, is that it?"

Dumas looked Renaud straight in the eye, and simply nodded. For the first time in many years, she was at a loss for words.

"We shouldn't have done it!" Renaud snapped. "We just couldn't wait, could we? We wanted to make things happen there and then, instead of going back to the beginning and starting again."

"That would have taken years," said Dumas. "We might still have been trying now if we hadn't added the extra cells to Genesis."

"Genesis?" Renaud was angry. "From what you've just said, it looks like we created a living time bomb inside those boys. If we can't reverse the progress of the reaction, we could be looking at a premature death, not just for them, but for the others we used the process on. That's not Genesis, Margherita. That's *Nemesis!* Do you realise what we may have done? We could have implanted a cell into their bodies which causes them to self-destruct. I don't know how, I'll have to see them, but what you're describing is some form of accelerated ageing process, and if it does become common knowledge, and they eventually *have* to go to a hospital, it *will* come out, be sure of it."

"There will be no hospital, Renaud, not for them, not ever, do you understand? You and I will do what we can, but there can be no hospital involvement. You and I will find a way to stop whatever it is that's happening to them. We created them, we can cure them. I must say though, that I like your description of what we may have created. A Nemesis cell! That has a nice ring to it. That's what we'll call it. We have to cure their Nemesis cells."

It was on hearing those last words that Doctor Alexander Renaud realised just how far apart he and Margherita Dumas had grown over the years. He knew so little of what she'd done since those days at the Clinique Sobel, apart from the fact that she was highly regarded by her peers and respected by all who knew of her pioneering work. On a personal level, aside from the fact that she had never once asked him about his marriage, or how his own career was progressing, she had all but excluded him from the lives of the two boys. Only now, when something seemed seriously wrong with their offspring, did she suddenly want his help.

In the car on the way to the house she shared with the boys, Dumas continued to talk of things that Renaud would rather have forgotten about.

"Just remember, Alexander," she said as they drove along the highway out of the city, "if it hadn't been for you and I separating, I'd never have had to dispose of the husbands. You must realise that I had to do that, because you weren't there anymore, and I wanted to ensure that the other boys all had a similar upbringing to our two. Alexei and Arturo grew up without their father being there for them, so I had to create the same circumstances for the others. You do see that don't you? You were never happy about what I did. You were too squeamish then, and I think you always will be."

"We didn't 'separate,' Margherita. We were never a couple! We worked together, that was all! There was no need for you to do what you did. For God's sake, woman, you murdered five innocent men, just so your experiment could proceed according to a revised set of parameters you'd drawn up. Why the hell did the others have to grow up like ours?"

"It wasn't just that," she replied. "Think of it, Renaud. What if, at any time, those boys had needed a blood transfusion, and their 'fathers' had volunteered to be the donor. What if for some reason one of them was subjected to DNA testing, and the truth came out and the 'fathers' realised that they weren't the fathers? It would have been hell, Renaud, absolute *hell* if they had found out. I should have had them killed years before, but I hadn't the resources. When the time came, I had to do it all myself, you chickened out from helping me, you lizard. You left it to a woman. I made it safe for us."

"Chickened out? Is that what you call it, when I simply refused to assist you in the murders of five men? There was no need to do it. If anything had ever come out about the boys' DNA, or their parentage, we could have claimed some simple error at the clinic. There was no need to kill them all."

"You fool! Even admitting to a mistake at the clinic would have destroyed my, *our* credibility, don't you see that? There was no other way."

Alexander Renaud knew there was no point in arguing with Dumas. He knew then that she had somehow detached herself from reality, had become totally wrapped up in the belief that what she, or rather *they* had done years ago at the Clinique Sobel was of such importance that the secret had to be protected at all costs, no matter what the expense in terms of human lives. She would kill to protect the Genesis Project, and he was certain she would kill to prevent knowledge of the so-called Nemesis cell ever leaking out to the world of established medicine.

As the car pulled up outside the entrance to the converted barn which was now home to Dumas and the boys, Renaud felt a sense of trepidation as he tried to envisage what he would find behind the thick, forbidding, heavy oak doors that formed the front entrance.

Chapter Twenty-Seven

Aberdeen, Scotland, July 1994

The St. Andrew Street building belonging to the Robert Gordon University's School of Life Sciences in Aberdeen housed some of the finest educational laboratories in the country. They contained a wide range of instruments enabling students to study a wide range of forensic applications. These included a varied selection of spectrometers, chromatographs, and DNA analysers. The building housed a dedicated forensic examination suite where specialist microscopes and document analysis equipment were housed, in addition to a room where crime scenes could be simulated for study.

It was in this building that eighteen-year-old Harry Houston began his university life, as he studied for the degree that would enable him to enter the Scottish Police College at Tulliallan Castle in the county of Fife. Once his degree was in his pocket, Harry could count on being part of the police force's accelerated promotion programme, and he could see himself as an inspector before reaching the age of thirty, perhaps even sooner.

No one was prouder of Harry on the day he began his new life as a university student than his father Angus, his objections to Harry's decision not to follow in his footsteps into the family business long forgotten. Angus and Margaret had driven Harry into Aberdeen and helped him settle into his room in the Halls of Residence, making sure that he had everything he needed for a comfortable beginning to his student life. Harry was keen to remind them that he was only forty miles or so from home, and would be seeing them most weekends, but, as parents are prone to do, they behaved as though Harry was going to be living a thousand miles away, and there were tears in Margaret's eyes as they drove away from the impressive building where Harry would be accommodated. Younger brother Duncan, who'd accompanied them to see Harry installed in his new lodgings, waved vigorously through the back window of the family's dark blue Ford Granada as the figure of Harry receded into the distance with every yard they drove. Now that Harry had officially left home, Duncan felt very grown up, and, as he was about to begin working part-time with his father in the butcher's shop, in between his studies, it seemed as if a whole new life was beginning not just for Harry, but for Duncan and his parents too.

Hardly a word was spoken on the drive home to Ballater, apart from Margaret's occasional references to items of trivia that she was sure Harry had forgotten, that she would send on to him, or wondering aloud if he would be warm enough at night, sleeping in a strange bed and all. Angus was quick to remind her that the Halls of Residence were equipped with central heating, and that Harry would probably be as comfortable as he'd ever been in his life, and she eventually fell silent when Angus chided her once too often for behaving like a mother hen that had just lost her favourite chick.

As for Harry, as soon as his parents and brother were gone, he lost no time in unpacking his clothes, hanging them in his new wardrobe, and placing his books and stationery items on the desk provided in his room. Then it was time for a tour of the facilities.

As he wandered round the various rooms and laboratories of the St. Andrew Street Building, Harry was like a child let loose in Santa Claus's grotto. His eyes took in every piece of equipment. He ran his fingers reverently over the polished shiny metallic surfaces of spectrometers and all the other paraphernalia that would be part of his life for the next three years. He made mental notes of those pieces of equipment with which he was unfamiliar, and which would require further investigation. He was determined to familiarise himself with every item he would be called upon to use in his studies, for Harry was resolute in his desire to succeed, to be the best he could in his chosen career, and he knew that his time at university would provide him with the biggest step forwards yet in his personal quest to achieve his ultimate dream.

That night, while some of the newcomers to the university took the opportunity to mix, mingle and introduce themselves to their fellow students over a drink or two in one of the many bars that thronged the streets around the Halls of Residence, Harry Houston sat quietly in his room, reading over and over again the prospectus of his degree course, his excitement building by the minute. He couldn't wait to start work!

Chapter Twenty-Eight

Zurich, July 1994

Renaud and Dumas crossed the wooden-floored hall of the converted barn she called home. Dumas's heels clacked on the polished slats that made up the floor, signalling their arrival to anyone in the house. The two of them walked up to a large door inset into the wall furthest from the entrance. Dumas turned the handle, and the door swished open as though on silent hinges.

"It's not locked," said Renaud, with a hint of surprise in his voice.

"They're big boys now," replied Dumas, "They don't need to be under lock and key any longer, like babies. They're totally trustworthy. They know the risk they would run if they leave this place without me, so, it never happens. Besides, they have everything they need right here. They have nothing to leave for."

Renaud followed as Dumas led the way through the door and along a hallway, hung with pictures of Adolf Hitler, Vlad the Impaler, (the model for Bram Stoker's famed Count Dracula), and the Russian Tsar Ivan the Terrible, all homicidal butchers of their fellow man. Renaud found it difficult to know whether the pictures were the choice of Dumas or of the young men with whom he was about to become reacquainted after his lengthy absence from their lives.

"What? No room for Stalin?" he asked in as jocular a fashion as he could muster, trying to ascertain whose choice the pictures had been, though he thought he knew the answer.

"You should know my thoughts on communism, Renaud. I wouldn't entertain any representation of that murdering socialist bastard within a mile of my home, or pictures of any other left-wing orientated socialist scum."

That answered Renaud's question perfectly, as if he hadn't already known. Doctor Margherita Dumas was without doubt one of the most extreme politically right-wing members of his profession that Dumas had ever met, and it was obvious that the passage of time had done nothing to mellow her attitude.

A few steps further, and they passed through another door to the room where the boys were sitting enjoying their favourite pastime, watching the television.

"Arturo, Alexei, I've brought someone to see you," said Dumas, and the two boys turned towards the door and both smiled as they recognised Renaud.

"Hello, Papa," they chimed in unison, and their smiles at seeing Renaud seemed genuine enough to him. His own feelings confused him. He thought he'd be over the moon at seeing the boys again, but instead, he felt a cool distance between himself and them, as if time and absence had collaborated to erect a barrier between them. Even so, he tried to be as friendly and as fatherly as he could.

"Hello, boys, how are you? I'm sorry it's been so long since we saw each other, but Mama must have told you that our respective schedules have kept us apart for some time."

"We're fine, Papa," said Arturo, "though Mama has explained that we may have a problem that you can help us with."

"You've told them?" asked Renaud of Dumas, trying to keep his voice as level as possible.

"They know everything about their conception and birth," Dumas replied. "It was imperative for the sake of their education and development that they be made aware of their background as soon as they were able to fully grasp the technical and biological details of the matter. They also know that they have a genetic defect that you and I are going to do our best to correct."

Renaud was stunned. He hadn't thought that Dumas would have been so forthcoming with the boys about their beginnings.

Dumas continued, "Their education is almost complete. They have learned everything I could teach them, and far more besides. In addition, I have conditioned them to be immune from the pathetic side of human emotion. They feel no falsely directed pity for the poor or the oppressed, as the bleeding-heart liberals of the world have us all do. They believe in the survival of the strongest and the fittest. They know that in order to survive and evolve, mankind must weed out the weak and the imperfect, and they are ready to do whatever we need them to do in order to prove the correctness of my theories. One day, we will recreate the Genesis Project, and that day might be sooner than you think, Renaud, if we can solve the enigma of the Nemesis cell."

"But what of the others, those from the Blenheim Wing experiment?" asked Renaud. "We used the same procedure, the same cells on them too. They could carry the same defect, and, if they do..."

"If they do," Dumas interrupted, "then we must do something to correct the situation. Don't you realise that if the problem is not correctable and the boys have a terminal condition, then one day they will go to a doctor? There will be scans and investigations carried out on them, and someone just might begin to put two and two together, and that, my good doctor, would prove disastrous for both of us, financially, professionally, not to say criminally."

Renaud looked hard at Dumas. He knew she was right, and yet, until he examined the boys and ascertained the nature of the defect, and exactly what was causing it, he refused to speculate as to what may or may not take place in the future. For now, he needed time, time to examine Arturo and Alexei, to study the results of the tests, and formulate a solid opinion on whatever had caused Dumas to call him to Zurich in such a hurry. She was, after all, a fully competent physician in her own right. She was equally as capable as he to make a diagnosis of the boys' problem. Then he thought that she probably already *had* made a diagnosis, one that probably scared the hell out of her, and she wanted him to confirm it, for better or worse. She needed him to provide confirmation of whatever ailed the boys, and she wanted him to help her to cure it, and, if they couldn't be cured...?

Renaud shivered at the prospect. Knowing Dumas as he did, he feared for the boys who now sat watching scenes of the genocide being carried out in Rwanda, where, between April and July, a million people, mostly Tutsi tribespeople, but also a great number of Hutus, had died in a vicious bloodbath of ethnic cleansing. They were still being conditioned to Dumas's way of thinking, being brainwashed into following her political beliefs to the letter. Though he had great sympathy for the boys, he felt that they'd been completely dehumanised by Dumas and her twisted beliefs, that they would never truly have a part to play in society. In short, whatever the current problem, whether he and Dumas could cure whatever had afflicted Arturo and Alexei or not, Alexander Renaud feared for their future. He couldn't see where they could fit into the world as it existed, or what sort of life Dumas had prepared them for.

The two doctors arranged to examine the boys later that evening, then, leaving them to continue watching the scenes of genocide on the flickering screen, Dumas and Renaud removed themselves to Dumas's office, where they spent the next few hours closely studying the meticulous records compiled by Dumas, which chronicled every day of the boys' lives, every cough, every sneeze, every medical procedure Dumas had carried out on them.

As he read over and again the history of the two boys in the room down the hall, Renaud was forced to relive in his mind the beginnings of the Genesis Project, and perhaps for the first time since those days at the Clinique Sobel, the knowledge of what he and Dumas had done now gave him cause to regret that Arturo and Alexei had ever been born.

Chapter Twenty-Nine

The following day saw Dumas and Renaud busily carrying out a whole battery of tests on Arturo and Alexei. When she had the barn converted into their second home, Margherita Dumas had ensured that like the house in Ostend, this one had a fully equipped infirmary and separate laboratory. She had already, as Renaud suspected, carried out a full sequence of tests on the boys, and had called him in when she required his confirmation of what she'd discovered. She needed to ascertain whether he could offer additional help and expertise in diagnosing exactly what had gone wrong and in putting together a programme to reverse the process that had begun in the boys' bodies. Only she and Renaud had the intimate knowledge that surrounded the secret of the boys' conception, and therefore only the two of them could do anything about the problems that now faced them.

Six hours after they'd begun, the two doctors left the boys to relax in their rooms while they conferred in the laboratory. It was Renaud who broke the silence that had fallen over the room as they'd completed the last of a series of diagnostic tests on blood, urine and tissue samples taken from the boys.

"I see what you mean, Margherita. For some reason, the original cells we inserted into the boys' initial DNA makeup, which should have been absorbed and assimilated into their bodies over time until they ceased to have any significance, have suddenly started to grow, at an accelerated rate. That should not have been possible."

"I know it shouldn't have been possible, but it's happening," said Dumas with an air of frustration in her voice. "The question is, what can we do about it?"

"The whole thing was your idea in the first place. You invented the process. Don't you have any theories?" asked Renaud.

"Only one," replied Dumas. "We used the additional DNA strand as an accelerant to ensure that the whole reproductive process worked. Before that, the cells kept breaking down and it was impossible to reach the point of successful implantation with a viable egg. The new strand, what we're now calling the Nemesis cell, was supposed to destroy itself after birth, or at least, as you say, be absorbed and rendered inert by the boys' bodies. I think that, instead of being destroyed or assimilated by the body, the cells simply lay dormant, and now something has made them active again. What we're looking at is a potential takeover of many of the body's normal cell structures and functions by the offshoots of the original Nemesis cells."

"But that would be potentially disastrous for the boys, and for the others who we created using the same process," said Renaud in horror.

"That's why we have to find a way to reverse the current level of activity by the rogue cells," Dumas continued.

"If the Nemesis cells take hold of the body, and continue to develop and act as they are at present, it will eventually lead to varied and catastrophic organ failures, and to irreversible brain damage. Before that, though, they would probably suffer from multiple carcinomas as a result of rapid cell growth and their bodies would be unable to fight the disease at all because of the presence of the alien DNA in their make up. Their higher brain functions would be impaired and they would probably go mad long before the brain reached a vegetative state," Renaud hypothesised.

"I know that already," a frustrated Dumas almost shrieked at Renaud. "As I said, the question is, how do we stop it from happening?"

"We need time, Margherita, we need time," Renaud said thoughtfully. "Whatever happens will be slow and gradual, so at least we have a window of opportunity in which to put things right. How much do the boys themselves know about what's happening to them?"

"They know everything," said Dumas. "I've always told them the truth about everything to do with their lives, and they had to know they were in danger. They took the news very well, and will co-operate in every way with whatever we have to do in order to reverse the actions of the Nemesis cells."

Renaud couldn't quite believe what Dumas had just told him.

"Everything," he gasped. "You told them everything?" Are you completely mad, woman? What if they decide to take it into their own heads to leave here and seek treatment at a hospital or other facility? What if they don't believe we can help them? If they were to spill the beans about what they know, about *what* they are..."

"They won't go anywhere or say anything Renaud, be assured of that. The boys know only too well what the potential consequences of leaving my care may be. They don't want to end up as freaks in a medical sideshow, and they also know that there is no-one in the world apart from you and I who knows their history and their physiology sufficiently well to even attempt to reverse the progress of what they now know is a potential killer inside them. Also, my careful conditioning over the years has made them unafraid of death, as you know. They are, I assure you, quite fatalistic about the possibility that they may not live long."

"I hope you're right, Margherita, I really do. Look, we'll let them rest after the tests, and try to start finding a way to beat this thing in the morning, agreed?"

"Agreed," nodded Dumas, and then added, "Alexander?"

"Yes?"

"I'm glad you're here, really I am."

"I never thought we'd end up working this close again Margherita. I just hope we can succeed."

"If we don't," said Dumas, "the whole thing will have been for nothing, the clinic, the women and the killings, all for nothing. We have to find the way to beat this Renaud, we just *have* to!"

Renaud barely heard her; he was already poring over her day by day medical diaries and his own notes, deep in thought, looking for the solution that just might save them all.

Chapter Thirty

31st December 1999, Aberdeen, Scotland

Police Sergeant Harry Houston sat at his desk, tapping his pencil on a blank jotter as he stared at the computer screen in front of him. He'd set the screen to show a countdown to the hour of midnight, when the world would celebrate the new millennium, the arrival of the year two thousand. Harry was quite happy to be at his desk that evening. He'd spent two days at Christmas with his parents at home in Ballater, and had enjoyed all the trappings of a typical family festive season. Now, as the New Year approached, he felt good to be back at his desk, doing what he did best.

Since leaving university armed with his degree in Forensics with Law, Harry had breezed through the training at the Scottish Police College at Tulliallan Castle in Fife, earning the 'baton of honour' as the top cadet of his entry, and had already made rapid progress in his career. He'd enjoyed his stay at the college, set as it was in almost ninety acres of mature woodland, reminding him somewhat of home. He loved the old castle which had been headquarters to the exiled Polish High Command during World War Two. Harry could sense the history of the place, and he felt at home there. He'd socialized in the bar from time to time, though he was known to all, students and instructors alike, as a studious, polite, and ambitious young man who never drank too much. Harry preferred to be in control of himself and his emotions at all times. He'd spent almost three years as a police constable, at first working with a tutor constable, an experienced officer whose job it was to help Harry settle in and learn the rights and wrongs of his new career. He'd earned his sergeant's stripes, and, following yet more specialised training at the police college at Tulliallan, had recently been appointed a detective sergeant. Now he found himself a part of the Grampian Police Force's Rapid Deployment Unit, a specialised task force set up to deal with unusual and dangerous situations and to handle the increasing amount of organised crime in the area. He loved the work, and especially the people he worked with, all of whom he would trust with his life. This evening, there were just two officers on duty in the RDU's control room and admin office, Harry and another sergeant, Denny Boyd. The two men had quickly become great friends, Boyd being ten years older than Houston, and a great source of help and advice to the younger man.

Boyd enjoyed the company of the bright and eager Houston, who was determined and single-minded in his desire to be a first class police detective, qualities that Boyd appreciated and welcomed. They shared many an off-duty drink together and often attended soccer matches together to watch Aberdeen play in the Scottish Premier League. Houston was also an able rugby player, and had soon found a place in the local police team's first XV, and Boyd would take whatever opportunities he had to go and watch his young friend play the game he loved but had never been any good at playing himself. Once a week Harry was a welcome guest in the home of Denny Boyd and his wife Lorna, who would prepare meals of such quality that Harry was sometimes ashamed to admit to himself that they were on a par with, if not occasionally better than, those prepared by his wonderful mother Margaret.

"Ten minutes to go," said Houston casually.

"Eh?" replied Boyd, who had been daydreaming lazily in his chair.

"Ten minutes until midnight, New Year, Hogmanay, a new millennium and all that," Houston droned.

"Oh, yeah, sorry, Harry, I'm knackered. It's been a long shift, and what with it being so quiet, it puts the old grey cells to sleep, if you know what I mean."

"I know. I can't believe how quiet it's been. It's like all the bad guys have taken the night off to celebrate with the masses."

"I'm just glad we're here in the warm, not like the poor buggers out there patrolling the streets, having to deal with the drunks and the prats making fools of themselves just because it's a new year."

"Wouldn't you rather have been with Lorna tonight?" asked Houston, suddenly changing the subject.

"Hell yeah, of course I would, but then who'd have wanted to volunteer to baby-sit the new boy eh?"

Both men laughed. Harry knew that Boyd had volunteered like himself to provide cover in the RDU control room this evening. Though no one seriously expected any major incidents on this night of all nights, someone had to be there to monitor the array of computer screens and be ready to respond to any incoming emergency situation that might develop in the Grampian area, which was prodigiously large.

"Lorna was OK about it," said Boyd, continuing the thread of the conversation. "She knows that at least next year the old man will be at home with her, so she's got something to look forward to, know what I mean?"

They both laughed again. It was standard procedure that no officer would be forced to work two holidays in a row, so next time a new year dawned, it would be someone else's job to sit in the office and watch the clock ticking inexorably toward midnight.

"Anyway," said Boyd, "She knows you're coming for dinner at the weekend, so she wants some time to herself to work out her next culinary masterpiece. She's got a real soft spot for you, Harry, you know that?"

"She always makes me feel right at home, that's for sure," said the younger officer.

"How long now" asked Boyd.

"Hmm?"

"Midnight, you fool, how long to go? My word, now who's dreaming, Harry boy?"

"Sorry, four minutes to go, Denny."

Both men fell silent for a few seconds, Harry watching the screen, tapping his pencil as before, and Denny Boyd hoisting his feet up and placing them squarely across his desk, enjoying the chance to relax in the company of his young friend and colleague. Hell, they were even being paid overtime for the dubious pleasure of being on duty in the dead of night.

"She thinks it's real, you know," said Houston out of the silence.

"Who thinks what's real?" asked Boyd. "Make sense will, you man?"

"My mother thinks the millennium bug is real. A real bug, I mean. I've told her about it so many times, that it's a computer threat, that things might not work quite right after midnight, but she's convinced herself that it's some sort of actual bug that has infested the world's computers and is going to eat all the 'little chips' as she calls them, some time after midnight."

"Go on! You're having me on," said Boyd with a huge grin on his face. "No one's that gullible, especially not your Mum, from what I know of her anyway."

"Honest, Denny, it's true. I know she's a lovely intelligent lady, but my Mum just has a blind spot where computers are concerned."

"When I meet her, I'll ask her," promised the older man. Then, "Do you think all this is going to come crashing down in a couple of minutes then?" he asked, pointing out the myriad computer screens around the room, each with its own terminal and keyboard below it, just waiting to be attacked by the so-called millennium bug.

"Nah, not at all," said Harry confidently. "The experts have all assured us that it'll never happen, haven't they? There might be one or two glitches here and there where they don't record the right date for a time, but apart from that I don't foresee any problems at all. Anyway, we'll soon know, two minutes to go."

As the two Scottish policemen prepared to welcome the new millennium in their office in Aberdeen, Lucia Cannavaro was preparing to do the same thing in her compact apartment in Turin, in the company of her son Angelo. Lucia was superbly proud of her son, who had proved to be of above average intelligence and ability throughout his academic years, and who was now fluent in three languages, and employed by the European Economic Community as a linguist, translating at various meetings for many of Europe's leading economists and politicians.

Her pride and her love for her son were matched only by her sadness at having to welcome another new year without Antonio by her side. It had been so hard to come to terms with being a widow at such an early age, and had it not been for the support and love she'd received from the handsome young man who now sat opposite her in her small but comfortable living room, Lucia really didn't know what she would have done. The strange thing about her son was that Angelo had grown to be such a well muscled and athletic man, and he was indeed a very handsome young man, but he had so little of his father's looks about him. Lucia would have taken even more comfort from his company if there had been a little bit of Antonio in his physical appearance, but she just couldn't see it. Strangely, there was something about Angelo that reminded her of someone, but she couldn't quite place who it was.

As the second-hand on the clock brought the new millennium ever closer, Lucia smiled at her beautiful son.

"Angelo, forgive for asking, my son, but, you are keeping up with your medication, aren't you?"

"Yes, Mama, of course I am. You made me promise, though I don't see why I should take those damned pills when there's nothing wrong with me. I feel fine, I always have."

"Please, Angelo. You know what the letter said. Do it for me, please, and for yourself. You cannot take any chances."

"Yes, Mama, Okay," replied the young man.

It had been three years ago that Lucia, in company with four other women around the world, had received an unexpected letter bearing the signature of Doctor Margherita Dumas. The letter had stated that, due to the experimental nature of the artificial insemination process they'd helped to pioneer, a small problem had been discovered in the ability of the children born from the process to regulate their own immune systems. It went on to explain that there was no imminent danger to the children, and that she and Doctor Renaud had developed a drug that was designed to counteract the breakdown of the immunity normally afforded by the body's own system. A box containing a year's supply was enclosed with the letter. One tablet a week was all that was required to ensure that the children, now all grown of course, would remain healthy. Like Lucia, the other women of the Blenheim Wing had all explained to their sons the history of their conception, and had no difficulty when it came to explaining the course of action they must take to ensure their continued good health. The young men all railed against the thought of taking the pills, but all acquiesced in the end. After all, it was just one a week.

There had been no return address on the parcel containing the tablets and the letters, but each year, without fail, another year's supply would be delivered to the mothers of the Blenheim boys, well before the previous supply ran out, and all the young men remained healthy.

Lucia and the other women may have thought it odd that Dumas had chosen this strange method of contacting them and sending medication through the post, but they all remembered the secrecy that had surrounded the process that had given them there sons, and knew better than to question this latest development. These annual deliveries were in fact the only reminder any of the women had ever had of their past involvement with the Belgian doctor. They accepted the news of their sons' weakened immune systems in good faith, and without exception they were all extremely grateful that the two doctors had gone to the trouble of developing a drug specifically designed to help their sons. The boys themselves, all young men by now of course, were dutiful sons, and all aware of the need to preserve their own health. Without fail, they all took their medication regularly.

Lucia had filled two of her best lead crystal wine glasses, part of a set of six that had been the last anniversary present Antonio had bought her, with the best Chianti she could afford. Now, as the clock struck the hour of midnight and a swell of cheering and clapping from the revellers in the street rose into the apartment from the square outside, the glasses made a satisfying 'chink' as she and Angelo toasted the beginning of the new millennium.

"Happy New Year, Mama," beamed Angelo, with a wide and warm smile on his face.

"A happy new millennium my son," replied his mother, adding, "And here's to the memory of your dear Papa, who would have loved to have been with us this night. May he rest in peace and his soul be forever blessed by our Sacred Virgin."

"To Papa," echoed Angelo Cannavaro, as the new millennium replaced the old century, and the world looked forward with optimism to a brighter and better future.

Zurich, 00.15 hours 1st January 2000

There were no celebrations to mark the millennium in the converted barn on the outskirts of the beautiful city of Zurich. There, in the well equipped sterile environment provided by the purpose-built and highly secret infirmary within the barn, two young men lay on hospital cots, intravenous needles running from overhead drips into their right arms, their eyes closed in sleep, as the latest attempt to preserve their lives gathered in intensity. Margherita Dumas slept little that night. She paced the floor of the laboratory, her brow furrowed with worry, deep in thought. She didn't want to do it. She didn't want to involve him any more, she wasn't sure how much she could trust him, but she knew that she would have to pick up the telephone in the next day or two, and call Alexander Renaud. She hated to admit it, but she needed him.

Around the world, the so-called 'millennium bug' failed to bite.

Chapter Thirty-One

Arturo and Alexei sat up in bed, smiling at Renaud. Dumas had called her former colleague four days before, being careful not to arouse too much suspicion in his wife, Marlette. It wouldn't do for her to think that Renaud was involved in anything deeply important or remotely sinister. Renaud had so far justified his trips to Switzerland by explaining to Marlette that his expertise in fertility treatment was often called upon by his old mentor and colleague, and that she often required his assistance with her latest experiments. He had told Marlette some, though not all, of the story of the Clinique Sobel, and she understood that he needed to maintain his link with Doctor Dumas.

Of course, Madame Renaud knew nothing of the darker elements attached to her husband's past, or of the murderous deeds of Doctor Dumas, with which her husband's life and conscience would be forever tainted. She did however partly share one secret with her husband, one that even the brilliant Doctor Margherita Dumas was unaware of, and that in itself gave Marlette sufficient motivation to encourage her husband to continue his occasional professional liaisons with his old friend and colleague.

"So, you are feeling better, eh, boys?" asked Renaud of the two young men, so alike they were indistinguishable from each other to the untrained eye. Renaud and Dumas were sufficiently adept at telling them apart after all these years, though no one else could have done so.

"Much better, thank you, Papa," replied Arturo. "Mama says you have solved the problem of the sudden proliferation of the Nemesis cells."

"Not solved, exactly, but the irradiated serum you've been receiving has acted as a barrier to prevent the division and multiplication of the rogue cells. It will give you immunity against further sudden attacks such as you've just experienced. We shall now set to work to produce the serum in an oral form, so that you may take a regular dose to maintain your body's stability."

"Another tablet, like before?" asked Alexei.

"Exactly," replied the doctor, "One a week, I hope, and you'll be as good as new."

"Thank you Papa," said Alexei.

"Yes, thank you," echoed Arturo.

"Why do we not see you so much anymore?" Alexei continued the conversation by asking a question that the two boys had asked many times before. The time between visits had over the years become increasingly longer, until Renaud rarely saw the two boys, except when Dumas invited him to occasional and intermittent meetings to discus their health and intellectual progress.

"I've told you before," Renaud replied, "that Mama and I no longer work together. I have another life at home in Belgium, with my wife, who you have never met, and I have work there also, which must be attended to. You must also remember that your Mama and I are no longer the close friends we once were, though we both care for you, and will always ensure that we do our best to look after your health and well-being."

"Why did you and Mama not marry each other?" asked Arturo.

"You must understand," Renaud continued, "that your mother and I were never in love with each other. We would have made each other very unhappy if we had married and tried to live together as well as work together."

"Hmmm, love, that stupid concept keeps cropping up in our studies of human behaviour and throughout the history of literature. Why do humans hang so much importance on the idea of such strong emotional ties between man and woman? It is not necessary to be 'in love' as you call it in order to procreate and ensure the continuation of the species. Strength of mind, of character, and the will to survive are surely the most important virtues to be sought in order to ensure the survival of any species. We are the prime examples of that, are we not, Papa?"

"Yes Alexei, I suppose you are," Renaud sighed, "but even you need the help of your mama and I in order to survive, do you not?"

"Only because the original procedure was flawed," snapped Alexei. "If Mama and you hadn't made an error all those years ago we wouldn't be in this situation today, would we?"

"That's true, but we can do nothing about that now. We must do what we can to ensure that you stay well, both of you, and I promise you that we will do everything we can, always."

The door to the infirmary opened, and Dumas breezed into the room.

"There now, what did I tell you?" she enthused at the two men in the beds. "Didn't I tell you that Papa and I would succeed in making you both well again?"

Renaud seethed inside at Dumas's attempt to share the credit for his work in rapidly diagnosing the latest problem being generated by the Nemesis cells, but he knew that Arturo and Alexei were so fiercely loyal to Margherita that they wouldn't have wanted to hear that just two days ago she had sat with her head in her hands in the laboratory, ready to give in to the seemingly insurmountable problem being caused by the rapid acceleration in the growth of the rogue cells within their bodies. She had tried and failed to halt the irrevocable advance of the Nemesis cells as they continued to assault the internal organs of the young men. They had both become ill very quickly, and she'd tried everything she knew to slow down the acceleration, without success. Even doubling the dose of the original drug that she and Renaud had devised for the purpose had had no effect whatsoever. She had been ready, as she put it when Renaud arrived, to 'terminate the experiment.'

Renaud had been the one who had sat quietly at the laboratory's central console and methodically worked out that the proliferation in the cells was being caused by the body's inability to produce sufficient antibodies to control the new and unexpectedly rapid advancement of fresh growth from within, and that the solution was relatively simple. The Nemesis cells, themselves the product of irradiated DNA introduced to the original cell matrix prior to implantation all those years ago, could, he hypothesised, be held in check by attacking them with a simple serum containing a new and stronger source of radiation. In other words, he wanted to build a radioactive barrier in the bloodstreams of Alexei and Arturo that would hold the Nemesis cells back, like a dam. He thought, and Dumas agreed when she realised he was talking sense, that a continued metered dose of the new serum would effectively stop the Nemesis cells in their tracks, by bombarding them with a stronger and more potent radioactive charge. Renaud was using strength to defeat strength, a little like the philosophy propounded so recently by Alexei.

Dumas continued where she'd left off. "Now, while you've been talking to Papa, I've been busy working on a method of turning our new serum into a solid form, to make it easier for you to take, and look, here it is."

The doctor held up a small white pill between her finger and thumb, as though it were a precious gem, a diamond of inestimable value, which as far as the lives of the two young men were concerned, it probably was.

"Just one of these, every week, and you'll be fine," she said, as though she had been the sole participant in the production of this new elixir of life.

Soon afterwards, the two doctors left the infirmary and retired to the laboratory once again. Margherita Dumas sat on a high stool, a cup of coffee in her hand, and relief washed over her as she looked at Renaud.

"We must try to ensure that this never happens again, Renaud."

"How can we do that? We have no idea of how or when the rogue cells will find a way past the new radiation barrier and begin attacking their bodies again. All we can do is be ready to act when and if it happens."

"I shall have to send a new supply of 'immune support tablets' to the women. I will tell them that that the formula has been changed to allow for the growth of their son into full maturity or some such story. We must ensure that those young men do not fall ill and gravitate into the hands of conventional medicos."

"Agreed," said Renaud, who added, "When I think back to those days in Belgium, I wonder what the hell we thought we were doing. I know we were young and idealistic, and we thought we could do what everyone said was impossible, but did we really think we could do this and get away with it forever? Surely someday someone will find out what we did. How can we hope to hide it forever?"

"We have done something that the world wasn't ready for, that's all. We have the satisfaction that no one else is even now any nearer to replicating what we achieved all those years ago. Not only that, but what I'm learning every day from Arturo and Alexei is helping to drive forward my research at the Strada faster than anyone would believe. Soon, Renaud, very soon, I will be able to recreate the original Genesis Project, but this time with the approval of the world's medical fraternity, and those two young men in the other room will have been my inspiration for that achievement. "

"You can't possibly be serious, Margherita! You mean you're going to do it again?" Renaud was aghast. "How can you even think of such a thing?"

"My dear Renaud," she said very quietly, "You will say nothing to anyone of what I have just told you. I am close, very close, to being able to move my research forward. Don't forget that the boys born to the women from the Clinique Sobel are all thriving and healthy, thanks to our medication and diligence. Not only that, but my sources inform me that since their fathers died, all have developed exactly as I wished them to, so that they are all now totally loyal to their mothers, and have developed a strong sense of individuality without sentimentality.

They are physically, emotionally, and intellectually superior to their fellow human beings, exactly as I knew they would be when we first began Genesis."

Renaud knew then that Margherita Dumas was close to losing her grip on reality. She couldn't be serious in thinking that she could go ahead with creating a second generation of children born with the defects present in Arturo, Alexei, and the sons of the women from the Blenheim Wing. And yet, Renaud knew that she was deadly serious, deadly to the point that he had no doubts that she would kill again. She had already killed five good and innocent men in addition to the Japanese financier, in order to engineer the lifestyle of the boys they'd created. She would kill again, and again, as many times as she thought necessary in order to protect her secret.

As he caught his flight back to Belgium the next day after saying his farewells to Alexei and Arturo, and armed with his own notes and a copy of the new formula for the life-saving drug for the boys on which he could base further work on the subject if he had to, Doctor Alexander Renaud vowed never to set foot in the converted barn near Zurich ever again, no matter the cost to either himself or the twins he'd left behind there. If he had to, he'd help Dumas with future problems, but she would have to come to him, to the old house, the one he still maintained for the rare visits by Dumas and the boys to Belgium, the house on the cliff tops, near Ostend, the house where the boys had been born so long ago, the house with the windowless rooms.

Chapter Thirty-Two

Aberdeen, August 2001

Harry Houston, Denny Boyd, and four of their fellow officers, all members of the Rapid Deployment Unit, left the lounge bar of the Caledonian Hotel on Union Terrace just after four p.m. The six officers had been celebrating the successful conclusion of one of their biggest cases for some time, and had left the office at police headquarters on Queen Street some two hours previously, ready to enjoy their off-duty time. Having drunk more than one toast to the success achieved primarily though the forensic knowledge and capability of Harry Houston, they now walked together to the end of Union Terrace to the junction where it joined Union Street, the city's long main thoroughfare. After much hand shaking and a few pats on the back for each other, they separated, each man going his separate way. Houston and Boyd were the exceptions, the two of them walking along Union Street to where Boyd's car was parked in Golden Square. Boyd had avoided drinking any alcohol, sticking to lemonade, so that he could drive the two of them to his home in the village of Cults, on the outskirts of the city, where Lorna Boyd was preparing a meal. As they walked they looked up in admiration at the glistening stone of the buildings that made up some of the finest architecture in the North-East of Scotland. To many people around the world, Aberdeen is famously known as 'The Granite

City' for the use of that material in the construction of many of its buildings. But to the locals, and many others, it is also known as 'The Silver City' because when the sun shines and reflects from the surface of the granite, it appears as if the buildings have been rendered with thousands of tiny, shining gems that glint and glisten in the light. This was one of those days, and the two men felt an immense pride to be able to serve the community in such a historic and beautiful city as this, and never more so than when they had concluded an investigation such as the one they'd just completed.

It had been Houston's instincts, helped by his forensic training at the University, that had led the squad to first suspect that a series of unfortunate deaths at the city's Royal Infirmary might have been caused deliberately. Though the patients had all died on different wards, over a period of nine months, something just didn't smell right to Houston. The police had been called in when the last patient involved, Flora Banning, had died after apparently making a full recovery from a heart bypass operation. Despite the doctor in charge issuing a death certificate indicating that the woman's death had been due to natural causes, her family had insisted on an independent autopsy being carried out, which revealed that a small but significant dose of insulin had been administered to the woman shortly before her death. Flora Banning was not a diabetic, and there was no reason why insulin should have been present in her body.

The doctor who'd issued the death certificate, Doctor James Darrow, immediately fell under suspicion, as he had attended Mrs. Banning throughout her stay in the hospital. The initial investigation could find no motive that would explain Darrow having administered what amounted to a fatal dose of insulin to his patient, and every member of the medical staff who had had access to the patient came under investigation.

The RDU were called in when the investigation began to stall for lack of credible evidence, and it had taken Harry Houston less than a week to put together a timeline of the questionable deaths, and link the patients involved with Doctor Darrow, who even though not directly involved with the care of each and every patient involved, had been on duty and in the vicinity of those patients' wards close to the time of each death.

That had been enough for the Procurator Fiscal, Scottish equivalent of the USA's district attorney, to issue an order for the exhumation of the bodies of four of the six victims. The other two had been cremated and were beyond the reach of the investigators.

As a result of the exhumations and the subsequent detailed autopsies, it was ascertained that insulin had been administered to all but one of the patients. In that one case, strychnine had been given to poor Davie Rowan, who, it transpired, was a diabetic, and already receiving regular injections of insulin. An insulin overdose would have aroused suspicions, hence the change of toxin.

Doctor James Darrow was now languishing in a cell beneath police headquarters, and Harry Houston was the undeniable rising star of the Rapid Deployment Unit. Promotion to inspector lay ever closer for the young sergeant, and he basked both in the warmth of the sun and in the pride of his recent triumph as he and his friend walked the last few yards to Boyd's car.

"You know, Harry," said Boyd, "It won't be long before you're an inspector, and then you'll no' be wanting to chat and drink with the likes of a mere sergeant like me, that's for sure."

"If you think that promotion'll go to my head, Denny Boyd, you can just forget it. I'll still be the same man as I am now, and I'll still be expecting my invite to dine each week. Otherwise, how will I ever survive?"

Boyd smiled, for he was only teasing his young colleague. He knew that despite his ambition and his ability, Houston was what was known as a 'coppers' copper'. He would always have his feet planted firmly on the ground, and he'd never forget a friend, or talk down to a junior officer. Harry Houston had two attributes that made him stand head and shoulders above many of his fellow men, and his fellow officers. He had integrity and reliability, and those qualities commanded respect from those with whom he worked, superiors and peers, not to mention the constables below him.

Denny Boyd wasn't sure exactly how far Houston was destined to progress in his career, or just what he was capable of achieving on an investigative level, but he knew that Harry's name and Harry's flame belonged on a larger stage. Boyd knew it, though he couldn't have foreseen at that time on just how large a stage Harry Houston would one day act out his tour de force, his big case, the one that would make his name, and his reputation.

For now though, the two men sat in quiet and mutual friendship as Boyd drove the few miles to his home, where Lorna had prepared a wonderful meal. The pair of them felt, rightly, that they had deserved every morsel they devoured that evening. Boyd drank a few whiskies, as did Harry, who eventually slept in the Boyd's spare room, as he had done on numerous occasions in the past.

The following day, the sun rose early, and after a hearty breakfast prepared by Lorna, Houston and Boyd drove to work together in companionable silence and Harry Houston, star of the moment, moved a little nearer to the next milestone in his rapid rise up the promotion ladder, and his date with the case that Boyd had dreamed would one day fall his way.

Chapter Thirty-Three

Brussels, Belgium, November 2001

Alexander Renaud walked briskly along the street towards his house. The leafy tree-lined avenue where the Renauds resided was a far cry from the cold and clinical world of hospitals, research laboratories, and medical decisions that made up the vast bulk of Renaud's professional life. He paused as he walked, taking a moment to look up at the trees that stood ramrod straight on both sides of the street, like soldiers standing to attention. In this case, the parade seemed to be incorrectly dressed, as the ravages of autumn had left most of the branches bare of leaves, so that the trees themselves appeared to be pointing imploringly at the heavens with their many twisted fingers, beseeching the sun to return and warm them, and to give them the renewed strength to revive and replenish themselves. The dark, overcast skies carried the impending threat of rain.

Renaud allowed his thoughts to wander in the direction of Margherita Dumas. He hadn't heard from her in some time, so he could only assume that all was well with Arturo and Alexei. He'd often mused over the strange twist of fate that had brought Dumas and him together. He'd been struggling for a year before he'd met her, trying to establish himself in the field of fertility research, without success. They'd literally bumped into each other at the bar of the Intercontinental Hotel in Frankfurt during a conference on the subject and had struck up not just a conversation, but a partnership of sorts. It had, of course, as he knew, always been a slightly one-sided partnership, with Dumas having had the finances and the business acumen needed to establish the Clinique Sobel, where the two of them had achieved so much together. Renaud had been young and idealistic, and prepared to take chances, cut corners, in short, do whatever was necessary to achieve what he thought was a perfectly legitimate goal. Only later, when things had begun to go wrong, and he'd realised the enormity and potentially unethical side to what they were doing, did he begin to have doubts about the partnership.

True, he'd done his best to distance himself from Dumas as the years had gone by, but he knew that they would always be linked by Arturo and Alexei, and by all that had transpired at the clinic. Yet, as much as he wanted to believe that he was innocent of the greater part of Margherita's crimes, he felt that if the truth were ever to come out he would find it hard to convince anyone that he hadn't been complicit in the fire that had destroyed the clinic, the death of a Japanese financier, and, worst of all, the murders of five innocent men, the fathers of the children conceived in the Blenheim Wing. There was no way that Renaud could ever reconcile those deaths in his mind. They'd been committed personally by Dumas in order to further her own twisted belief that she could dictate and modify the personalities of the boys by altering the circumstances of their lives. It was psychological manipulation of the very worst kind, but who would believe that he'd had nothing to do with it?

As he reached his house and walked up the steps that led to his front door, he thought briefly of the secret that he'd kept from Dumas all these years. What would she do if he were to tell her of his deception all those years ago? Would she understand why he'd done what he had? Of course not! He knew that without a doubt, and he shivered at the thought of what Margherita Dumas would do if she were to discover his long-buried secret. Even his dear wife Marlette was unaware of the gravity of the deception to which she was unwittingly a part. She knew some, not all of what he'd done, but the exact truth was his alone to know. Even Marlette wouldn't truly understand if he told her everything, but she knew enough.

Renaud turned his key in the lock and the door swung open to admit him. The warmth of the inside of his home was a welcome relief to Renaud after the chill autumn air that had accompanied his walk along the street. He quickly hung his coat on the rack beside the door, shook off his fears and worries, fixed a smile upon his still-handsome face and called out;

"Marlette my darling, it's me, I'm home."

Chapter Thirty-Four

The Strada Institute, Zurich, December 2001

Margherita Dumas hunched over the papers on her desk, deep in thought. Here, in the peaceful and private surroundings of her palatial office at the institute, she was free to worry if she wanted to, to panic even, without anyone prying into her innermost thoughts or witnessing what she perceived as a great weakness. She was, after all, a coldly calculating and clinical exponent of the various arts at which she'd become adept.

Medically speaking, she was of course a genius; she needed no one to tell her that. What she'd achieved so far in her career had been nothing short of breathtaking, and her expertise and talent for advancing the boundaries of her research were becoming legendary. Various research establishments around the world relied on her and her institute for confirmation of their own research, or as a consultant whose reports were seen as vital in establishing the credence of many new and radical procedures.

Margherita Dumas had other, less savoury talents which those who held her in such high esteem would have been astounded to learn of. She was an accomplished and skilled killer, her mind being inventive to the point of genius in devising ways of despatching those who she considered a danger to herself or to her less than legal and highly unethical research projects. She had proved to herself on more than one occasion that her proclivity for murder was matched only by her steely will and single-minded determination to succeed in proving herself to be superior to her peers both professionally and personally.

Dumas looked up from her papers, and her right hand reached across to open the bottom draw on that side of her desk. She moved the pile of papers that resided there and pulled from beneath them a file, pale yellow in colour, and tied with plain wax-coated string. Untying the precise bow that held the file closed, she quickly removed a faded photograph that sat at the very top of the file's contents. Her face softened as she gazed at the face that stared back at her from the grainy black and white image in her hand. The handsome man in the photograph was dressed in the unmistakeable black uniform of an officer in Adolf Hitler's feared SS, the death's head insignia quite clear even though the photo was crumpled and faded. The smile on his face was warm and compassionate, and in his arms he held a baby. There was something else in that face, yes, there was pride in his eyes as he held that tiny infant close to his chest.

Margherita sighed as she placed the photograph down on her desk, and she thought of her father with a fondness born of childhood memory, of the man who had guided and taught her during those first, important years of her life. Doctor Karl-Heinz Fleischman had held the honorary rank of colonel in the SS, and at the time of his daughter's birth he had been posted to the concentration camp at Chelmno, near the town of Kolo in Poland, where he had worked under the brutal camp commandant Hauptsturmfuhrer Hans Bootman. Chelmno was the first of the Nazi death camps to have used poison gas as a means of extermination, though it wasn't clear whether Fleischman had been a part of that gruesome ritual. With Bootman's approval, Fleischman had carried out a number of experiments on the inmates of the camp, experiments that his daughter had taken upon herself to continue in later years, though using modern medical techniques and without the unnecessary suffering imposed on the victims of her father's work.

As the defeat of Germany loomed large, Fleischman gathered his wife and baby daughter and fled the country, going into hiding for over a year until resurfacing in the Belgian town of Charleroi on the River Meuse, under the assumed name that Dumas now bore. Helped by a network of Nazi sympathisers, he had taken the name of a Belgian worker from Antwerp who the Germans had transported to a work camp early in the war and whose family had been wiped out in 1941. Fleischman, now Dumas, kept a low-profile during his years in Charleroi, working as a simple orderly in the local hospital whilst teaching his daughter all he could at home, thus giving the young Margherita a thorough grounding in his perverted philosophies. Fleischman had died in a motoring accident when Margherita was just twelve years old, but his influence and his teachings had never left her, not for a single day. When her mother passed away in Margherita's eighteenth year, the young Dumas, newly ensconced at university, had inherited all of her father's papers, not to mention a large sum of money, and her future was assured.

Margherita Dumas easily qualified as a doctor in her adoptive country, and her brilliance propelled her into the world of research, where she soon gained a reputation as a quite superb though at times unorthodox student of all things new in the field of human fertility treatments. It was her strange and at times unsettling attitude to her research that eventually caused some of her contemporaries to question her methods, and eventually led the young Dumas to open her own research facility, which later became the respected Clinique Sobel.

Sighing loudly, Dumas replaced the photograph in the file which held the personal memories of her father, her mother, and her life from her own birth, re-tied the wax string that held the whole thing together, and replaced it in the drawer, turning the key in the lock and placing it in her purse, where it would remain until she felt the urge to gaze at her father's face once again.

Feeling more confident once again, Margherita Dumas found a new level of concentration, and returned to the problem she was previously grappling with, namely, the new infection that had beset Arturo and

Alexei. The burning question in her mind at that moment was whether to go it alone, to try to find a way to combat the new and dangerous development that had caused her such consternation, or should she pick up the telephone and call Renaud, on the basis that two minds addressing the problem may prove better than one?

As if it could give her the answer she sought, she turned to look at another photograph, this time a framed picture on the wall behind her desk. In answer to anyone who asked about it she explained that it was photograph of her cousin's two sons, pictured sitting together leaning against a substantial oak tree. The picture of Arturo and Alexei served to remind her, if she needed any reminding, of what it was she sought to achieve in the world, and, as she concentrated her thoughts on that image behind the glass, that desire to create the perfect specimen of humanity gave Margherita Dumas the answer to her quandary.

Chapter Thirty-Five

Aberdeen, Summer 2003

Detective Inspector Harry Houston looked across his desk at the attractive woman who sat in the visitors' chair. Houston was not yet fully accustomed to the lofty position of his new rank, and felt slightly uncomfortable with the task he had to perform. The powers that be had decided that he needed an assistant in his new role as the front-line head of the force's new in-house murder investigation unit. The unit had been set up as a specialist team that would involve police officers, forensic scientists, scenes-of-crime officers, and administrative back-up all under one umbrella, able to work together without the need for constant inter-departmental referrals, enabling, in theory at least, a faster initial incident response time and an even faster detection rate.

When Chief Superintendent Archie Dalgliesh looked for an officer capable of pulling this team together, he selected Detective Chief Inspector Donald Burnett, the former head of the RDU, as the ideal candidate. Burnett, given a free hand to appoint the best men and women he could find to make up the team, then proceeded to elicit more than one set of raised eyebrows within the force by selecting the newly promoted Houston to be his right-hand man. Surely, many experienced officers on the force thought, he should have chosen one of them, someone with the years on the job that such a position called for. Burnett, however, was adamant. He wanted Houston, who, with his second-to-none detection rate since joining the force, and with his knowledge of forensics and the law, was the ideal choice in his book. Burnett got his way, and Houston got the job.

Not that anyone resented Harry or begrudged him his good fortune. Everyone who had met or worked with Harry Houston held the young inspector in high regard. He was easy to get along with, knew what he was talking about, and perhaps most importantly of all, there was that mutual respect that seemed to follow Harry around, given and received, that never failed to endear him to people.

Houston looked again at the young woman, who now crossed then uncrossed her legs, fidgeting slightly in her chair.

"Er, sir," she said, "Are you actually going to say anything, or do I just sit here until you decide whether to give me the job or not?"

"Eh, oh, sorry, sergeant," Houston replied, as though emerging from a daydream. "I hope you'll forgive me, I was just thinking that here I am, hardly in the job for two minutes, and now I'm having to appoint a sergeant to work with me when I was one myself not that long ago."

"I know, sir," replied Sergeant Debbie Forbes. "I can always come back another day if you'd prefer it, sir."

Houston spent a moment or two mentally appraising the fair-haired five-feet-two-inch tall detective sergeant in the immaculate navy blue trouser suit before continuing. "No, no that's all right. Look, Sergeant Forbes–Deborah, may I call you Deborah?" She nodded. "I've read your file, and I've talked to people you've worked with, and you're the best damned candidate for the job. If you think you can work with a DI who's a fair bit younger than you are, and you think we can get along together, the job's yours."

"Forget the age, sir. I've found out as much as I can about you too, and I know you're good at what you do, so, if you want me, it looks like you've got yourself a sergeant."

"Right then, Deborah", said Houston with authority, "I'll let Mr. Burnett know, and we'll arrange your transfer.

"Thank you, sir, and there's just one thing. If we're to work closely together I should tell you that nobody calls me Deborah any more. It's just Debs, or Debbie if that's ok with you."

Thinking of his own Hamish/Harry name, Houston replied with certainty. "Debs it is then. Off you go now, Sergeant, and I'll see in a few days."

Debbie Forbes left the room, Houston relaxed in his chair, and, though neither of them knew it at the time, a partnership that would prove a highly redoubtable one in the fight against crime in the city of Aberdeen and the North East of Scotland had been born.

Chapter Thirty-Six

Ostend, Belgium, Autumn 2003

Alexei and Arturo sat passively on the sofa, their eyes seemingly glued to the screen of the widescreen television in the corner of the room. They were watching the movie *Schindlers List*, and were intently viewing the scenes of cruelty and deprivation being carried out on the helpless victims of Nazi aggression and racial cleansing. On the surface, not much had changed since the days when, as young boys, they'd watched television in this self-same room, studying the many and varied ways that mankind had devised throughout history to inflict pain and suffering on each other. Now, though, there was a subtle difference. The two men no longer had need of such images in order to learn; now they watched them as a means of achieving a perverse gratification, for both men now harboured an intense desire to enact the very scenes they watched on the screen.

In the office on the other side of the wall from where they sat, Dumas and Renaud were involved in a discussion that Renaud especially would rather have wished to avoid; though for him there was another reason for his wish, one as yet unknown to Dumas. "You bloody fool, Margherita, you stupid bloody fool," said Renaud with an intensity that was almost frightening to Dumas. She'd never heard him speak to her in such a tone before. "I told you all those years ago that we were playing with fire, that no one could predict what the effects of irradiating the DNA would be. Now you tell me that they're going to die, and there's nothing we can do about it! On top of that, they'll go mad first, and turn into the pathological killers you've always wanted them to be, and you won't be able to control them! What sort of monsters are they becoming, for God's sake? What sort of monsters are *we* for creating them?"

"Be quiet, you idiot," stormed Dumas. "We can't turn the clock back. What we must do is minimise the effects as much as we can. Every test has shown that the process which began when the Nemesis cells began to override the boys' natural cell structure will take some time before it finally recodes their genetic make-up and we have to do what we can in the meantime."

"How long do we have before their organs begin to degenerate?" asked Renaud.

"When they reach the age of thirty, in a few months' time, their cell proteins will begin to change irrevocably. They will begin to experience headaches at first, as the first brain cells begin to alter and die, and then soon afterwards, the internal breakdown will begin. Tumours will spread at a rapid rate and begin to attack the major internal organs. The body's natural defences will hold the assault of the rogue cells back for a while, but as the Nemesis cells multiply and start to replace the body's own cells, the boys' immune systems will grow weaker and weaker until they can no longer function."

"And how long before they reach the terminal phase?"

"A year, two at the most." Dumas spoke almost matter-of-factly, as though the impending suffering and death of the two lives she had brought into the world mattered little to her.

"Damn you, Margherita, we have to do something. We can't just sit back and let them die."

"What do you suggest? I've brought them back here, to the place they were born, to make it easier for you to attend and assist me in devising a way to slow the process down, but believe me, I've spent the last six months in Zurich doing extensive and exhaustive tests, and I guarantee to you that my prognosis is correct and accurate."

"And the others," said Renaud with panic rising in his voice. "The boys from the Blenheim Wing at the Sobel, what about them? Will they suffer the same symptoms and inevitable end as Arturo and Alexei?"

"There can be no doubt of that. We've held the whole process at bay quite successfully for a number of years with the drugs we've provided for them all, but we can do nothing to stop the Nemesis cells now that they've reached their critical maturity level."

"So what do you suggest?" asked Renaud. "Do we tell the mothers? Do we do something to try to help them as we try to help Arturo and Alexei? The others are younger; they won't reach the same stage for a couple of years yet. We might make a breakthrough if we work at it together. Surely we *must* do something for them! You've kept me in the dark for months now as you struggled with this by yourself in Switzerland. Now you bring them here when it's almost too late. Tell me what you intend to do. I ask you again. Are you going to tell their mothers?"

Margherita Dumas was silent for a few moments as Renaud finished his almost hysterical diatribe. When she spoke again, there was coldness in her eyes, and a steel-like determination in her voice as she said to Renaud, very quietly, but with a terrifying edge to her words, "Tell their mothers? Oh no, Renaud, my good and sincere old friend, we are not going to tell their mothers. That, my dear Alexander, would be the last thing on this earth we would do."

Renaud's mouth fell open as the enormity of her words sank into his brain. Though she hadn't said it, he had no doubt what Margherita Dumas had in her mind, and his terror grew in the silence of that room, there where it had all begun in the house on the cliff tops, with the incessant sound of the air conditioning whirring in his ears, and the muffled sound of the television seeping through the walls into the office from the room where the two men who bore his genes sat in their familiar and sterile windowless environment, with the spectre of agonising death stalking them with every passing minute.

Chapter Thirty-Seven

Police HQ, Queen Street, Aberdeen, December 2003

Detective Inspector Harry Houston sat at his desk as evening approached. Houston was in reflective mood. His team was rapidly making a name for itself, thanks to his own leadership and intuitive detective skills, allied with his background in forensic studies, and the sheer tenacity and never-say-die attitude of his fellow officers. As well as the redoubtable Debbie Forbes, Houston had managed to unashamedly steal his old friend Denny Boyd from the RDU and had also recruited some of the finest officers in the North-East of Scotland to his team, namely Detective Sergeant Alan McNally, a dour but highly intelligent investigator, and his two detective constables, Andy Forester and Mary Dunblane. Forester was young and full of enthusiasm and had shown resilience beyond his years in his career to date. Mary Dunblane was a year or two older than Forester, but, with a degree in Mathematics and Computer Sciences gained at Heriot-Watt University in Edinburgh, she was the brains of the team.

The deceptively pretty young officer ran the logistical support functions of the unit with a professionalism that belied her years. Houston would swear to anyone who asked that Dunblane was on personal terms with every single byte that made up the computer's memory. In fact, he thought she was probably linked to the machine herself; such was her empathy with the thing. Every shred of information or intelligence that was gathered by the team, together with input from all external sources, was logged by Dunblane, and she'd devised programmes that enabled the team to link with other forces and exchange information on a scale far in advance of most police forces in the UK at that time. She could often obtain information from sources Houston could only marvel at, and though he suspected she might be using skills more akin to those of the hackers he'd heard plenty about, he preferred not to ask. Dunblane was good, bloody good at her job, and that was enough for Harry.

At least half the male officers in the headquarters building had probably tried to date Mary Dunblane at some time since she'd arrived on the team, but she'd steadfastly refused all offers, and she'd rapidly earned the reputation of being untouchable. Mary Dunblane was said to be married to her work. That was the way she liked it.

So this was the hand-picked squad that Houston had assembled, and they were doing a damn good job so far. They were rightly proud of their achievements. They had cut their teeth on a fairly routine murder investigation involving a newly burgeoning protection racket that had sprung up in the city's Chinese community. After a number of arson attacks on numerous Oriental-owned restaurants in the city of Aberdeen and its outlying suburbs, the situation had reached boiling point when a chef in the Golden Dragon restaurant had been found in the smoking ruins of his kitchen, with a six-inch kitchen knife embedded in his back.

Though it was first thought that the chef had been a victim of the racketeers, it transpired that he was in fact in the pay of the criminals, and had been caught by his employer trying to set the fire that had burned down the Golden Dragon. Knowing that he would be able to make a lucrative claim on his insurance policy if his restaurant were torched illegally, the restaurant owner had callously killed the chef, and then finished the job for him by setting light to the kitchen himself and allowing the fire to destroy his business.

It was the work of the blue-eyed computer whiz-kid Mary Dunblane that brought the team the clue that would eventually lead to them cracking the case. Checks on the dead chef led her to records in Hong Kong, where she learned that the chef was related to one of the families involved in the Aberdeen protection racket. Armed with that piece of information, Houston and his team were able to build a case against the biggest oriental crime syndicate in the city, and in addition to solving the murder, they were able to hand information to the Serious Crimes Unit that enabled them to close down the protection racket and arrest the major and the minor players in the syndicate's reign of terror.

Then followed the case of Martin Fergus, the notorious Stonehaven Strangler, who killed three women in the space of two weeks in the early autumn of that year. The little fishing town just a few miles south of the city of Aberdeen was rocked when three young married women were brutally slain, apparently without motive, all being found with the cords of their own dressing gowns tightly wrapped around their throats in a ligature of death. No suspects were evident in the series of crimes until a chance remark by a shopkeeper to Denny Boyd, to the effect that he'd seen two of the dead women walking together on the harbour wall, arm in arm, just days before their deaths, led Houston and his team to investigate the relationship that may have existed between the three dead women.

The three grieving husbands were questioned and re-questioned, the forensic evidence checked and re-checked, and a small filament of cloth from a woollen necktie discovered in the hair of Anne Scott was enough for them to link Fergus to the death of the second victim. Debbie Forbes felt that the women might have been more than just a little friendly, as she delicately put it. She thought she'd discovered the motive for the deaths. Houston concurred, and Fergus was brought in to the station "to assist the police further with their inquiries." Under questioning by Forbes and Boyd, (Houston thought Forbes, being a woman, might be the key to getting him to talk), Fergus soon cracked and revealed that he'd discovered his pretty wife Lorraine had been involved in a lesbian affair with Scott, and then later with Carrie Moses, victim number three. Furious with jealousy, Martin Fergus had first killed his wife, then systematically stalked and murdered the other two women. Neither Scott nor Moses knew of each other's affairs with Lorraine Fergus, nor did they know each other, so neither of them suspected that Martin Fergus had been the killer of his wife. Had Moses known of Lorraine's affair with Anne Scott, she might have suspected that she was next on the killer's list of victims. Sadly, she knew nothing until it was too late, and her body was discovered, like the others, naked and grotesquely posed on her own bed, by her husband when he returned home from work. Houston and his team had solved their second case in quick succession, and their reputation as diligent and effective crime fighters was growing with each passing day.

That reputation would be tested to the full by the numerous cases that came their way in the ensuing months, and each success that Harry, Debbie and the others scored in their fight against those who dealt in death added to the Murder Investigation Unit's prestige. Harry knew that very soon, if things carried on like this, his personal star would rise so high hat he would be expected to accept promotion to the rank of Chief Inspector, as was the usual case with graduates such as himself, yet he knew that he had found his niche, his forte. He was an investigator, a hands-on criminalist; he would never sit behind a desk handing out orders to others who would do the hard work on the streets. Whatever it took, Harry Houston was determined to remain at the "sharp end" of police investigation, and at that moment he knew that he would have a fight on his hands for the rest of his career. A fight not to rise through the ranks, but to stay where he was. The pressures would be enormous to advance to higher rank, but, just as he had single-mindedly stuck to his original desire to be a police officer, now he would stick just as firmly to his wish to remain a detective inspector. This, after all, was what he did best!

Houston smiled at his team as they all prepared to leave the office that night. It was Christmas Eve, and, with everything quiet in the city and no active cases on their books at the time, Harry had given them all two days off for Christmas, with orders not to show their faces in the office until December 27th. There was a spirit of camaraderie and goodwill amongst the small yet select team of officers, and even Mary Dunblane joined in by allowing the male officers the pleasure of the smallest of kisses as she wished them all a Happy Christmas. True to form, she was the last of the team (apart from her boss) to leave the office that night. She seemed almost reluctant to shut down her beloved computers, as though they would be lonely and miss her while she was away.

"Merry Christmas, sir," said Mary as they parted on the steps of the headquarters building.

"You too, Mary," smiled Houston as he made his way to his car, which was parked next to that of Denny Boyd, who was waiting for him in the car park. It was time for one of those special meals at the Boyd household before he made his way to Ballater, and the home of his parents for a typical Houston Christmas, turkey, veal, haggis and all!

Chapter Thirty-Eight

Zurich, Spring 2004

Alexander Renaud was a worried man. The summons from Margherita Dumas had sounded urgent, too urgent to be ignored. He'd made his excuses to Marlette before boarding the first available flight from Brussels to Zurich. He'd arrived late in the evening, too late to go directly to Dumas's office at the institute. He had no intention of visiting her at her home. Their relationship had become somewhat strained, and if it weren't for the boys, he would have refused her imploring call to come as soon as he could. Renaud knew that Margherita was no longer trustworthy.

After checking in at the Coronado Hotel on the outskirts of Zurich Airport, he'd showered and changed before eating a sparse meal in the hotel restaurant. He'd barely tasted the food, excellent though it was, as his mind refused to concentrate on anything other than the problem of Dumas and the boys. There was another reason, of course for Renaud's trepidation, but he knew that he could never reveal that secret to his former partner. The danger such a revelation could bring was too great. He knew that she must be getting progressively desperate in her search for a means of arresting the degeneration in the condition of Alexei and Arturo. In truth, Renaud had been doing almost nothing else for the past six months in his own laboratory, built behind his well-equipped surgery and clinic. He'd never be a Margherita Dumas, of course, for Renaud was happy to work in close harmony with his local community, to be a doctor who was respected by his patients as being kind, thoughtful and caring, whilst carrying on his own research in the lab.

As he retired to bed that night, he knew that the futures of the boys, (as he always thought of them, even though they were now adults), and others besides, would hinge on whatever solution or conclusions he and Dumas would reach over the next few days.

The following morning, feeling reasonably refreshed after a night's sleep and a good breakfast, Renaud left the hotel bright and early, travelling the twelve kilometres to the city along the A20 in the company of a silent and morose cab driver, who did nothing to add to his reservoir of good cheer, which was running increasingly low. Renaud wondered if the man behind the wheel realised that his sullen and grim-faced attitude was hardly conducive to receiving a large, or in fact, any sort of tip at the end of the journey. He considered the slightly amusing thought that the driver could probably give a lecture tour in the art of being miserable, and Renaud couldn't wait to be dropped off at the entrance to the Strada Institute.

Dumas was waiting for him as he was shown into her office, seated behind her desk with a perturbed look on her face and a deeply furrowed brow. "Alexander, so good to see you," she lied, barely able to conceal her contempt for the man who sat opposite her.

"You too, Margherita," Renaud lied in return. "Let's not waste time, please. Tell me what it is that's so urgent you couldn't tell me about it on the phone."

"I know you've been working on the problem also, Alexander. You must have been. Have you achieved any success?"

For a moment, Renaud suspected that Dumas had discovered his own secret, but then he realised her concern related only to solving the problems of Alexei and Arturo. With a sense of relief he replied in a surprisingly firm and confident voice. "I've given the problem much of my attention for the last few months, but the solution just won't come to me, Margherita. With all of your resources here at the institute I would have thought that you'd have found a way of slowing down or arresting the spread of the Nemesis cells by now. After all, you *are* the genius of this relationship, are you not?"

Dumas didn't fail to recognise the sarcasm in his voice as her face took on a look that barely disguised her dislike of the still handsome doctor with whom she had once worked so closely.

"Bah, you talk childishly, Renaud. My genius or lack of it is not the question here. If we cannot stop the spread of the cells, then we must assume that Alexei and Arturo will soon be entering the terminal phase of the condition, and that the same fate awaits those born as a result of our little experiment in Brussels all those years ago. You know of course that we cannot allow that to happen."

"Allow it to happen! What the hell do you think we can do about it? We have to do the sensible and the right thing now. We should inform the authorities, allow the best brains in medical science access to our notes, tell them what we did, and see if they can come up with a solution to the problem. It's the very least we should do for the boys and for those we caused to be born with this curse within them."

"The least we can do, you say? Are you absolutely mad, Renaud? If we admit to what we did in Belgium, then the very least that will happen is that we will both lose our licences to practice medicine. More than likely we would both end up behind bars for a long, long time, and everything I have built and worked for all my life would be destroyed. Don't you understand that if my process can be perfected, as I'm working on here, I stand to make more money than you could ever dream of? There are corporations, even nations, who would pay a fortune just to get their hands on half of what I've achieved so far."

"That's it, then, is it?" Renaud snapped at her. "Money, all to do with money. Don't you care about Alexei, Arturo, and the others? We caused them to be born like this, we made them what they are, and as for you, I even went along with your crazy plan to educate them yourself, to brainwash them with your wild theories about human emotions and the meaning of life as you see it. You made them devoid of feeling for their fellow man, and now you show the same scant disregard for their futures. You've made them into little more than animals; intelligent ones to be sure, but animals nonetheless, trained to do whatever you tell them to do. Be truthful, Margherita, what freedoms have you ever given them? They go where you say, when you say, they're only allowed outside when you give them your approval, and they have no free will of their own. They've never had the chance of self-determination at any time in their lives."

"Sentimental claptrap, that's all you can give me? Animals you say? Well, yes, in a way that's what they are, they're laboratory specimens, after all. We made them, created them from nothing, and they have responded to my training as I expected they would. Yes, they are totally receptive to my will, and whatever freedom I choose to grant them is gratefully received by the pair of them, as it would be by a faithful dog. Why on earth would I give them self-determination? They belong to me, Renaud, don't you forget that, they are mine, to do with as I please."

"How can you say that when they are a part of you, a part of me? We gave them life, you and I; they sprang from your womb for God's sake..."

"Enough!" shouted Dumas. "That's enough! They are *not* my children! We used my womb as a receptacle for the embryos we created, nothing more. It was a growing medium, a place to nurture them until they were ready for the world. As for you, you've always been too sentimental, too attached to them. You've wanted to treat them as sons, but they're *not your sons*, Renaud, are they? You know exactly what they are."

"Yes, I know what they are, and I also know who they are, Margherita. They might not be my sons in the true sense of the word, but they're more, much more than that and you know it!"

"I tell you, they are an experiment! To be human means having a father and a mother, the use of sperm to inseminate the female, the coming together of reproductive fluids in order to generate the chemical reaction that leads to fertilisation. Where was the sperm when they were conceived, Renaud, tell me that. They are the result of a scientific procedure, they have no father, and no mother, remember that!"

"You twist the truth. They may have no father in that sense, but they have something more. They do not possess the cells, the brains, the bones and the blood of both of us, but whatever you may think, you *are* their mother, the only one they've ever known. We remixed the genetic matter together, both of us. They are as much you as they are me, and we have to do something to save them, even if it means exposing our dreadful errors of thirty years ago."

"You are a romantic fool, Renaud; I should have known that you were incapable of seeing it through to the end. I always knew this might happen, but you wanted everything to be so nice, so right, so perfect, didn't you? They are going to die Renaud, painfully and horribly, and so are those we produced after them. It is up to me to see that we are not exposed to the consequences of the growth of the Nemesis cells. No one must ever know of the rogue cell's existence, Renaud, no one at all! Now leave me, I shall see to what has to be done. You are of no further use to me or Alexei and Arturo. They will follow my instructions. They know the truth of their genesis and they are only too aware of what is happening to themselves. They will protect me and the secret of their birth no matter what the cost, you may be assured of that, and in doing so they will protect you. Don't forget that, Renaud, for you will join me behind bars if word of this should become known."

Renaud knew that Dumas had finally gone over the edge. She had become a runaway train, set on a path to inevitable destruction, and he also knew that there was little he could do to stop the process of that annihilation without causing irreparable damage to himself and his family at the same time. There followed a further ten minutes of pleading and attempts to reach her sense of logic and humanity before, at last, Dumas appeared to mellow a little.

"Alexander," she said in the softest of voices, "We have been friends and colleagues for too long for it to end like this. Surely we both want what is best for all concerned in this matter. Let me make you a promise. You will return to Brussels, and I beg you to continue your researches there while I do the same here. There is still a little time before the rogue cells turn critical and the final stage of the termination begins. We may have missed something, you and I, there might yet be time to discover a way to slow the irrevocable march of the Nemesis cells long enough for us find a way to halt them altogether. We should never give in, not you and I. We have come too far together. Please, Alexander, go home to your wife. We must both do what we can, and no final steps will be taken without consulting you. That is my solemn promise to you."

Though unsure whether to believe in the apparent sincerity that now attached itself to every word that poured from her mouth, Renaud was prepared to clutch at straws in his attempt to stave off what he saw as an impending disaster that would engulf everyone concerned with the experiments at the Clinique Sobel. With a heavy heart, but with an optimism born of his own desperation, Alexander Renaud nodded and reluctantly acceded to Dumas's request. The two former colleagues parted on the coolest of terms, with Renaud uncertain as to where the road they had first trod together thirty years ago would finally lead the two of them and the two men who now sat in a room a few miles away from the institute, slowly counting off the days to their own demise.

Chapter Thirty-Nine

Turin 15th March 2006

"Happy birthday, my son," said Lucia Cannavaro to her beloved Angelo. Lucia was so happy to have her son with her so that they could celebrate his twenty-ninth birthday together. Since her own family and her late husband's parents had passed away some years ago, she'd tried so hard to make sure that Angelo's birthdays and any other special occasions with a family connection were treated with due respect and celebration. She knew the two of them had a very special bond, one that was stronger even than the usual mother and son relationship she'd read so much about in women's magazines.

"Thank you, Mama," laughed Angelo, as he swept her up into his arms, swinging her around and around until she was almost dizzy.

"Enough, Angelo, enough, please, my head will fall off soon," Lucia giggled.

He relented and placed his mother gently back down on her feet.

"I have something special for you this year my son," said Lucia as she handed Angelo an envelope.

"Now, Mama, I hope you haven't been spending all your money on me again. You know it's not necessary. Being here with you, sharing a meal together is all I need for my birthday."

"Since you got your own apartment, I don't see you half as often as I would like. I know you have your own life to lead and that's as it should be, but don't you dare to tell your mother that she can't spoil her only son on his birthday. That would be too unfair."

"I'm sorry, Mama, I'm grateful for whatever you've bought me, you know that. I just worry about you, and you should spend whatever money you have on yourself."

"Angelo, Angelo, don't you give me enough already? Every month you give me a portion of your wages, and you don't have to, but I love you for it, so don't you go lecturing me about spending my money. Now, please, open your gift, before I lose my temper with you, you naughty boy."

As his mother laughed and attempted to scowl at the same time in mock anger, Angelo Cannavaro carefully opened the envelope his mother had presented him with.

"Oh Mama, how wonderful!" he exclaimed as he removed the precious piece of paper from the envelope.

"I know you love the theatre my son, and I also know that you particularly want to see that play. I hope it's as good as you want it to be."

"There's only one ticket Mama, why don't you let me get another and we could go together?"

"Angelo my darling boy, you know very well that I'm just not a theatre person. I never have been. I don't understand half of whatever is happening on stage. No, please, you go and enjoy your play, and I will be happy for you if you come and see me the next day and tell me what a good time you had."

Angelo hugged his mother, and planted two kisses on her face, one on each cheek. He knew that the ticket in his hand was for one of the best seats in the house, and that his mother had probably spent a week's housekeeping money on it, just so that she could give him a birthday present that she knew he'd enjoy. He also knew when it was best not to lecture his mother any more on her having spent the money. Lucia was a proud woman, more so as she'd brought her son up virtually alone since the untimely death of his father.

"Thank you, Mama. Thank you so much. I will have a wonderful time. It is rumoured to be the funniest stage play seen in the city for ages. I love you very much. You are just too good to me."

"Enough now, Angelo, come, sit down I've prepared your favourite supper for you, and we have a fine wine to go with it. It isn't your birthday every day, you know."

As Angelo and his mother sat down to enjoy the simple meal of pasta and fish she'd prepared to celebrate his birthday, similar celebrations were taking place around the world. In New York, Tilly Garrelli sat with her son Peter in the Savannah Restaurant on East 48th Street enjoying a birthday lunch that Tilly had saved up to pay for over the last three months. Peter was happy and grateful, knowing the sacrifices his Mom had made over the years to help finance his upbringing and education. Why, that very night, Tilly would be back at work on the late shift in the all-night drugstore near her home, where she'd worked for nigh on ten years. In Zurich, Hans Todt and his mother visited the cinema, as did the Hammonds in London. The only exception to the mother and son get-togethers was the Dunne family. While his mother sat at home in Ireland, Patrick Dunne was somewhere in the North Sea, serving on board the oil rig supply vessel *Arctic Wayfarer*. As the hours of his birthday ticked away, Patrick was on duty on the bridge of his ship as she ploughed through heavy seas on her way back to Aberdeen from her latest voyage, carrying supplies and equipment to the rigs in the Brent offshore oilfield. Patrick knew that his mother would phone him on his mobile telephone that evening, and that a card would undoubtedly be waiting for him when he returned to his flat in the city of Aberdeen later that night. So it was that with the exception of Patrick Dunne, who had no choice in the matter, the men who'd been born as the result of the research and ingenuity of Doctors Dumas and Renaud at the Clinique Sobel over a quarter of a century earlier spent their twenty-ninth birthdays in the cheerful and joyous company of their loving and adoring mothers. Neither they, nor their doting mothers, could have had any inkling of the devastating events that were soon to overtake them all.

Aberdeen, 15th March 2006

As the night of celebration across Europe and in the New World drew to a close, and as Patrick Dunne oversaw bridge operations as the *Arctic Wayfarer* nosed her way through the waves towards the sanctuary of Aberdeen's harbour at a brisk twenty knots, Harry Houston and Debbie Forbes sat in the warmth of Houston's office quietly reviewing the strangest case the team had so far been called upon to investigate.

Debbie Forbes had called it The Case of the Dead Salmon, though Mary Dunblane had enigmatically and (to her mind) humorously logged it on her computer records as A Fishy Death. When Simon Carlisle, a man of some wealth and standing from the town of Windsor in Berkshire had been found dead lying next to an equally deceased salmon of huge proportions on the banks of the River Dee not far from the brand new Craigevar Hotel near the picturesque little town of Banchory, about eighteen miles from the city, Houston and his team were called in to solve the puzzling case. The case was made more baffling by the simultaneous disappearance of American businessman Carlton Ryder, who had been staying at the same hotel, and who hadn't been seen since the day of Carlisle's death. At first, it was thought that both men may have been the victims of foul play, but, when it was discovered that Carlisle and Ryder had been fiercely contesting the river for over a week, with both men determined to catch Auld Robbie, a salmon of some repute among the local populace, Houston had immediately suspected that the American might not be lying dead in the river or on its banks as was poor Carlisle.

When fish scales matching those of the dead salmon on the river-bank were confirmed as being present in the hair and on the skin of the deceased, Houston was certain of his theory. Sergeant McNally and Constable Forester began a systematic check of all departures from Aberdeen airport and the ferry terminal, and when these proved fruitless they widened their area of search to the rest of Scotland. Mary

Dunblane contacted the major English police forces, and so began a nationwide hunt for the American.

In the end, it was the American's penchant for using his credit cards that were his undoing. Thanks to Dunblane's timely warning to other forces to be on the lookout for the American, he was discovered when he used his Amex card to pay a hotel bill at the Ashford International Hotel in Kent, prior to attempting to abscond across the Channel to France, from where he would doubtless have boarded a flight to the USA. At the request of Harry Houston, the Kent police held the runaway stateside steel magnate until Houston and Forbes travelled the length of Britain to question and eventually arrest him.

Ryder soon confessed that he and Carlisle had been involved in a friendly competition to see who could catch the largest fish during their stay at the upmarket Craigevar. When told of Auld Robbie by the staff at the hotel, they both vowed to be the man to bring the local star of the river back to the hotel for the chef to cook. Twice, Ryder had the fish on his line (he said), only for the salmon to escape, and his misery was made more abject when Carlisle later hooked, landed, and stunned the fish in a matter of minutes as they sat fishing together on the banks of the beautiful Dee.

Taunted by Carlisle over his failure to hang onto the fish when he'd had the chance, Ryder had simply snapped, and had risen from his fishing stool, walked across to the other man, picked up the monster salmon and swiped Carlisle across the head with it. He swore he hadn't meant to kill Carlisle, but as he fell sideways from Ryder's blow with the fish, he'd fallen against the rocks that littered the banks of the river at that point. Carlisle died instantly.

"They don't come much stranger than that one sir, that's for sure," Forbes uttered with a wry smile on her face.

"Aye, death by salmon," quipped Houston, "and it wasn't even in a tin! I ask you, Debs, the things some men will do out of a sense of macho stupidity. The whole thing was quite simple really, once we got a hold on the salmon issue."

"I know, sir, but really, was it worth a man's death?"

"Of course not, but then, I really do believe that Ryder never meant to kill Carlisle; hurt him a bit, yes, but not enough to kill."

"So the rocks were just in the wrong place at the wrong time then," said Forbes.

"Yes, or maybe Carlisle and Ryder were in the wrong place at the wrong time."

"Yes, of course, sir, you're right. It looked a real mystery to begin with, but you had it sorted in no time at all really."

"*We* had it sorted Debs, the whole team. We work together; I couldn't have done it without the rest of you."

"Thanks sir," smiled Forbes. "Speaking of the team, Denny will be back from leave next week, then we'll have a full squad on line again. I hope he enjoyed himself, sunning himself on the beach in Tenerife."

"Oh, he and his wife will have had a great time, Debs, be sure of it. Now get yourself off home for the night, I'll see you tomorrow."

"Aye sir, I will, and don't you be too far behind me. You look tired."

Houston nodded, and yawned in agreement with his sergeant.

"Goodnight sir," she called as she left Houston sitting with his feet on his desk, getting sleepier and more exhausted by the minute. "I mean it, you go home too, get some sleep."

"I will. Don't nag though, there's a good girl."

"Okay sir. At least after the salmon we can't possibly get another case as weird and quirky as that for a while."

Debbie Forbes' footsteps reverberated down the deserted hallway of the Queen Street Police Station as she made her way to the elevator that would take her to the ground floor. Ten minutes later, Harry Houston followed in her footsteps as he too made his way home to catch up with some much-needed sleep.

Though neither of them knew it, their next case was to prove more baffling, far reaching, and humanly tragic than that of the case dubbed by their colleague Mary Dunblane as The Fishy Death.

Part III

FINAL REVELATIONS

Chapter Forty

6th June 2006, Turin, Tuesday

Angelo Cannavaro was warm, and just a little drunk as he made his way home after a satisfying evening's entertainment. The performance at the theatre had left him in a happy mood. The comedy had been just the thing to lift his spirits after a hard week at the office. Following the play, a few drinks in the bar had given Angelo a warm glow inside, and he'd forsaken the use of a taxi to walk the kilometre and a half to his home on the Via del 'Orzo. The bit where the leading lady had tripped over the feet of the doorman and gone headlong across the stage, collapsing into the arms of her mother-in-law, had been particularly amusing and Angelo laughed softly to himself as he replayed the scene in his head. Angelo would enjoy relating the funnier parts of the play to his mother when he saw her the next day, and he would of course thank her again for the wonderful birthday present. His seat that evening had been in the upper circle, close to the boxes where the wealthy would sit, and Angelo wondered exactly how much his mother had sacrificed in order to pay for his ticket. As he walked, he felt a warm glow pervading his entire being, a happiness born of the love he knew his mother had displayed in purchasing his ticket, and the wonderful memories he would have of the evening. Perhaps that was why he neither saw nor heard the man in black who stepped out from the alleyway less than a hundred metres from his apartment block, at least, not until the man spoke.

"Excuse me, please, but are you Signor Angelo Cannavaro?" the man asked, speaking in English.

Without thinking about it, Angelo answered, also in English, which he spoke fluently through his work as a linguist employed by the European Economic Community, Agricultural Affairs Division. "Yes, I'm Cannavaro, but what...?"

He never finished the question. As soon as he heard Angelo begin to reply in the affirmative, the man seemed to move with the speed of a cobra striking at its prey. The blade in his hand moved in a blur of speed and buried itself in Angelo's chest, and was removed again in less time than it had taken Angelo to speak his last few words. Knowing his aim to have been true, the man in black didn't wait around to see the results of his deadly handiwork. He quickly turned and disappeared down the street, and was long gone by the time Angelo's slumped and lifeless body was found in the entrance to the alleyway ten minutes later by a passing carribinierri patrol. Thinking Angelo to be a drunk asleep on the ground at first they had tried to rouse him, and only realised they were dealing with something far more serious when his body was turned over and the massive bloodstain on his shirt front and on the ground underneath his body was revealed.

At home in her tiny but clean apartment, Lucia Cannavaro was just going to bed, and her thoughts were looking forward to the next day, when she would see her son and hear all about his night at the theatre. As she lay her head on the pillow she could hear the sounds of sirens in the distance, police and ambulance she guessed by the different tones, and she felt sadness that someone's evening had ended in the need for such assistance.

Friday, 9th June, 2006. London.

John Hammond was twenty-nine, athletically built, and a computer whiz-kid much beloved by his employers at Selectronics Industries. An avid sportsman in his spare time, he was on his way home from a weight-training session at the gym when he was accosted by the man in black after parking his car in his garage. "Mr. Hammond?" asked the man as John fumbled in his pocket for his house keys.

"Yes, can I help you?" said Hammond.

It was enough for the man in black. The highly polished blade flashed in the moonlight, and in one swift movement John Hammond was despatched with exactly the same dexterity of hand as Angelo Cannavaro had been three days previously. He died in seconds, bleeding out on his own drive, just yards from his front door. His body was discovered by a friend an hour later, as he arrived to collect John for a game of squash.

The following morning, the police officers who knocked on Elizabeth Hammond's door brought her the news of John's seemingly senseless murder, and her world fell apart.

3rd July, 2006. Aberdeen.

The deaths of Angelo Cannavaro and John Hammond were unknown to Inspector Hamish (Harry) Houston and his team until some days later, when he was appointed to investigate the murder of Patrick Dunne in the city of Aberdeen on Monday, the third of July. Even then, the deaths of the two men in Milan and London didn't enter the equation until later, when the beginnings of a mystery emerged.

As Houston and his unit were soon to discover, Patrick Dunne, son of Theresa, had been working in the off-shore oil industry in Aberdeen for many years, first on the oil rigs that were serviced by the port of Aberdeen, and later, having undergone the necessary seafaring training, on the ships that supplied them. At the time of his death he was employed as first mate on the *Arctic Wayfarer,* a larger than usual oil rig supply vessel. His body had been discovered on the dock beside his ship by two of his shipmates who'd gone to search for him when he'd been late keeping an appointment for a drinking session with them in the Bridge Bar on Bridge Street in the city. Situated just off Union Street, the city's main thoroughfare, Bridge Street is no more than a five-minute walk from the harbour, and the berth of the *Arctic*

Wayfarer. Knowing Patrick's love of good beer, they'd wasted no time when they noticed he was an hour late, and set off to find him. He'd been stabbed, just once, through the heart, and had bled profusely, his blood dripping over the side of the dock and running in tiny rivulets down the harbour wall to stain the blue-green waters of the harbour a deep magenta as the colours of blood and seawater mingled together. His shocked crewmates had called the police, and it was only a short time later that Houston and his team from the Murder Investigation Unit arrived on the scene.

There were no witnesses to Dunne's death. The lonely dockside had been deserted when his unknown assailant had carried out the murder, and Dunne had died without anyone seeing or hearing anything. Houston, Forbes, and Boyd surveyed the murder site as the scenes of crime officers and forensic team made a painstaking search and examination of the body and surrounding area. After giving them time to do their jobs without undue interruption Houston approached Doctor George Murdoch, a recent but firm friend with many years as a police surgeon under his belt, and asked for his opinion.

"Nasty one, Harry," said Murdoch, "Single stab wound to the chest, pierced the heart, in one thrust. Whoever did it knew what he was doing, all right. I'd say you're looking for a professional."

"And the murder weapon?" asked Houston.

"A knife, obviously, but what kind I can't say until get him to the lab. I'll tell you this, though, it was no fish filleting knife that did this. It was sharp, long, and very, very deadly."

Twenty-four hours later, George Murdoch presented Houston with his preliminary findings, and he had a small surprise in store for the inspector. As he'd suspected, the knife was about six inches long, with a double-edged blade, honed to incredible sharpness, so that the entry wound was less than half an inch at its widest point. The surprise he kept till last however was that the body of Patrick Dunne contained traces of a powerful and lethal toxin, as yet unidentified, which Murdoch assumed had been injected into the victim via the surface of the knife. In short, Patrick Dunne's killer had been taking no chances. If the stab wound to the heart hadn't killed him, the poison sure as hell would have.

"Knife killings are usually personal," Houston said as he conferred with Forbes and Boyd. Like Houston, they were both skilled and professional investigators, and their recent successes since the squad had been formed forged a bond of trust and openness between them that transcended rank. In short, Harry Houston had made sure that his team knew that they were free to speak their minds, and voice their opinions about any aspect of a case if it helped lead to a solution. He trusted his fellow officers implicitly, and he knew that they would listen carefully to his words before voicing those opinions, which wouldn't necessarily agree with his, but that was the point of freedom of speech in Houston's mind. He might be the boss, but that didn't mean he was always right. He needed their input, and welcomed whatever they had to say, but for now, he was in control of the conversation.

"But there's something different about this one, I can feel it. If it were personal, why go to the trouble of impregnating a blade with poison? A normal run-of-the-mill killer would surely just have used the blade, and probably stabbed him more than once to make sure of the job."

"I agree sir," Forbes replied. "I'm sure this was a professional hit, though why anyone with big time connections would want to kill a second mate on an oil rig supply ship is a mystery to me. He doesn't seem to have had any history of criminal activity, certainly he had no record. He was only twenty-nine, seems a real waste to me, sir."

"All premature deaths are a waste, Debs, every one of them."

"True, sir, but we'll get to the bottom of it."

"We'd better. I don't want some contract killer wandering around the city thinking he can make fools of us, sergeant."

"Maybe it was drugs, sir", said Boyd, who had found no difficulty in adjusting to Houston's elevated rank. "We know that some of these guys on the ships are involved in the trade."

"Okay, Denny, you take that route, see what you can find out."

As they left the scene of Patrick Dunne's murder, the team was confident that they would find a motive and a solution to his killing before too long a time had passed.

Unfortunately, the more they tried, the more they failed to find a motive for the killing. Dunne had no close family in Scotland, no known enemies, and everyone seemed to have liked him, unusual in his line of work, but true nonetheless. No one had a bad word to say about the dead man.

Early on Thursday morning Debbie Forbes burst into Houston's office waving a piece of paper in her right hand. "Sir, you've got to see this," she said in a state of agitated excitement, pushing the paper at her boss across the desk.

Picking up the paper, Houston looked at it and then, with a slightly quizzical look on his face, he spoke to his assistant. "Okay, Debs, it's a picture of Patrick Dunne. What am I supposed to say?"

"But that's just it, sir. It isn't Patrick Dunne! This came through on the wire from Scotland Yard a few minutes ago. Mary had to confirm with them that it wasn't a mistake, then she passed it to me. They're looking for information regarding the murder of a man named John Hammond last Friday, and this is *his* picture."

Houston was stunned. The man in the picture he held in his hand was the double of Patrick Dunne. The hair, the eyes, the facial features were identical. They could have been twins, except for the fact that Dunne had no brothers or sisters on record, no family at all apart from his mother. From the information on the sheet provided by Forbes it appeared that Hammond had a similar family background to Dunne. In other words, his mother aside, none at all. The hackles on the back of Houston's neck began to rise. He could smell something fishy, and it wasn't coming from the docks!

Houston called the rest of the team into his office, where a hasty case conference was convened. The only one missing was Denny Boyd, who was still delving into his drug-related theory somewhere in the city, though Houston now felt that that particular avenue was rapidly looking like a dead end. Looking over his boss's shoulder at the remarkable picture, Forester whistled through his teeth,

"Well, it looks like the same guy, that's for sure," he said quietly.

"It doesn't fit, it just doesn't fit," said Houston.

"How do you mean boss?" asked Forester.

"I'm not sure, Andy, but I've got an itch somewhere in my head that I just can't scratch. There's more to this case than we're seeing, and I wish I could put my finger on it."

"Something'll break soon sir, I'm sure of it." This from Alan McNally, who was the quiet one of the team. "I'll be talking to Dunne's shipmates again later. Maybe they know something they're not telling us. You know, it's possible he and this other chap were twins, and were separated at birth or something, and then adopted by different people. It could happen you know."

"Then check it out, sergeant," said Houston.

"Aye, sir," replied McNally, and nodded to his boss as he left the office.

Across the room, Mary Dunblane began typing information into her computer, and created a new file that was to grow larger than she could have imagined.

"Okay, Debs. Get onto the Yard, tell them what we've got here, and send them a picture of Dunne. I think there's a need for a bit of co-operation between forces here, don't you?"

"Agreed sir, I'll get onto it right away. Mary, I'll need your help to get the information off to the Yard."

As Forbes and Dunblane began collating the information together ready to transmit to Scotland Yard, Houston sat deep in thought. Something was nagging at the back of his mind, an inkling that this case wasn't going to be quite as straightforward as any of them imagined.

New York, Saturday 8th July, 2006

Peter Garrelli never knew what hit him. The young English teacher had just sat down to lunch in his favourite diner, enjoying the first day of the weekend after a week surrounded by the hubbub of children's voices and the perpetual reverberation of sounds that made up the day to day life in a busy school, when the man wearing a hooded sweatshirt sitting in the booth behind him turned, smiled and asked, "Excuse me, but aren't you Peter Garrelli?"

"Yes, do I know you?" asked the teacher. A look of surprise began to form on Garrelli's face but before it had fully manifested itself, the man in black swiftly reached across the back of the seat and his blade sliced straight into the heart of Peter Garrelli, who slumped in his seat, as though asleep. The killer rose, left a few dollars on the table to pay for his meal, and walked calmly out of the diner, allowing the body of Garrelli to be found a minute later by the young waitress who'd served him, who, as was to be expected of a sixteen-year-old doing her best to earn a few dollars at her Saturday job, screamed the roof down. She screamed, and screamed and screamed, and it took the owner of the diner a full ten minutes to calm the girl down, so that, by the time he phoned the police, the killer was long gone, and of course, no one had heard or seen anything. This was New York, after all.

Harry Houston was ignorant of the death in New York as he liaised by phone and internet messenger with his counterpart at Scotland Yard, a Chief Inspector Ron Shackleton. Though Shackleton outranked Houston, the mutual respect for each other's professional positions ensured a smooth and co-operative dialogue between the two officers. The two men shared everything they had on their respective cases (which wasn't much), and it was Debbie Forbes who had the bright idea of trying to find out if there'd been any similar cases elsewhere in the past. Mary Dunblane even e-mailed Interpol.

Twenty-four hours later both Scotland Yard and the Grampian police were made aware of the death in Turin of twenty-nine year old Angelo Cannavaro. They were even more stunned when his picture was forwarded to them by the police in Turin. They'd added another link! Cannavaro was, (or at least could have been) the identical twin, triplet, whatever, of Dunne and Hammond. There was not one visible difference between them. The police officers in London, Aberdeen, and Turin were incredulous at this latest development in their respective cases. So far they were all ignorant of happenings in New York and would be for some time. For the moment the police forces of Europe were left to blunder along in the dark, devoid of clues, witnesses, or evidence in their hunt for what was looking more and more like a serial killer, or, worse still, an international conspiracy involving more than one killer. Even more mysterious, of course, was the fact that the victims were all identical, and it wasn't long before the police were calling for an in-depth forensic study of the remains of all three victims, with priority being given to DNA sampling of the dead men. Luckily, because of the fact that they were murder victims, the bodies of all three men had been preserved in the respective morgues of the cities where they'd died, and the examinations proceeded post haste.

The results of those examinations were startling to say the least. Inspector Houston sat with his chin cradled in his hands, looking quite mystified as he conversed with Sergeant Debbie Forbes.

"It's just not possible, Debs," said the inspector, exasperation in his voice. "How on earth can three men who as far as we know have never met, and lived in different countries, with different mothers and fathers, all have identical DNA? And that's another thing, all their fathers have been dead for years apparently. Their mothers appear to be their only living relatives."

"Not only that, sir," said the sergeant, "but absolutely *everything* about them was the same, hair colour, eye colour, shoe size, physical build, you name it, they were like peas in a pod. It's as if they were the same person. McNally phoned a while ago, by the way, there's no evidence of any of the men having been adopted so that knocks that theory on the head."

"I didn't think he'd find anything like that, Debs, but it was worth checking out. Something about this case gives me the creeps, I can tell you that."

Houston was bemused by the baffling murder, and the identical victims that had been identified in different cities around Europe. So too were Shackleton in London, and the police in Milan, where Captain Enzo Berlini was leading an elite team of investigators with instructions to crack the case. Unfortunately, as time went by, and no further information was forthcoming, frustration and a sense of failure began to enter into the hearts and minds of those trying to solve the mystery. Two weeks after the murder of Patrick Dunne, a routine internet flyer from the New York police department, originally sent to Scotland Yard and forwarded to him by Shackleton, found its way via Mary Dunblane's computer onto Houston's desk, and the Scottish inspector found the ongoing mystery suddenly compounded by the sight of a picture of Peter Garrelli staring up at him from the flyer.

Now the case had become one of transatlantic proportions, and the various heads of the police forces involved called a conference, to include the chief investigating officers from each of the victims' countries. It was decided to hold the meeting at Scotland Yard, and a few days later the officers involved gathered in a conference room on the fourth floor of the headquarters of London's Metropolitan Police. It was decided that Houston be appointed the co-ordinator of the investigation team, and that the others would continue their investigations, but would report any and all findings to the Scotsman, who would collate a record of the ongoing investigation, giving the team instant access to whatever information they might glean. Harry was pleased to be given the task of heading the team, and left with high hopes that he and his team together with the resources of the other forces involved would soon begin to piece things together.

* * *

The men's mothers had all been interviewed, and though they all seemed reluctant to divulge too much to the police, this was taken as a sign of the shock and associated psychological trauma each woman was undergoing at the death of their respective sons. No, of course they didn't know who would want to harm their sons, no, they didn't know these other men whose pictures they were being shown, and no, they couldn't explain the physical likeness or the DNA results. Though the police had some doubt about the women's veracity, they could think of no reason why they would lie or impede the investigations into their sons' deaths.

Another two weeks were to pass with no progress being made by any section of the international task force, as the members of the various teams had come to refer to themselves. It took another death to bring them a little closer to an answer, and this time, they felt they had a clue of sorts. They had a witness!

In point of fact it was the Swiss police who had a witness. A man by the name of Hans Todt had been seen leaving his office at his usual time of 6 p.m. on Tuesday night. As he crossed the road, the doorman of the building saw a man approach Todt, speak briefly to him, then watched, horrified as the businessman fell to the ground, leaving the doorman in no doubt as to what he'd seen. The strangest thing about the doorman's testimony, however, was that he'd sworn to the Swiss police that the man who'd carried out the attack was none other than Hans Todt himself, or rather, a man who appeared to be his exact double! Herr Gruber the doorman would not be shifted from his testimony despite initial police scepticism, and only when the police checked for similar slayings in recent times and found the Interpol record of the worldwide investigation into the identi-murders, as they'd become known to the international team of investigators, did they realise that they might be able to provide a breakthrough of sorts in the case.

Chapter Forty-One

Zurich, Thursday 3rd August, 2006

Three days later, Houston and Forbes sat in the comfortable office of the head of Zurich's homicide investigation division, Commissioner Claude Borgo. The Swiss detective was pleased to be offered the assistance of the Scottish inspector and his sergeant, and had done everything he could to make them feel welcome on their first visit to his city.

"So, inspector, tell me what you think of this strange case we have on our hands."

"Well sir," replied Houston in deference to the Swiss detective's rank, "the longer the case goes on the more mysterious it gets. With this killing though, we've got the beginnings of a breakthrough, I'm sure of it. My sergeant and I have a theory. It's a bit of a wild one, but our fellow officers around the world think we may be onto something."

"Please go on, inspector," said Borgo, a large, rotund, but very alert man who obviously knew what he was talking about, and who gave the impression of not suffering fools gladly.

"Clones, Commissioner!" stated Houston, emphatically. "Both my sergeant and I are of the opinion that someone, somewhere has succeeded in cloning a human being, and the murder victims are all the product of some as yet unknown scientific experiment."

"That's right, sir, we've considered every logical and illogical possibility, and cloning seems to be the only thing that would explain how all these men share the same DNA, and the same characteristics in every physical respect," added the sergeant.

"Well," said Borgo, breathing deeply and exhaling as though a great weight had been lifted from him, "I have three things to say to your theory, inspector. One, as no one has as yet succeeded in cloning a human being doesn't mean it hasn't been done, or that it's impossible to do so. Therefore, your theory has possibilities. Two, if you wish to find out more about the likelihood of such a thing having been achieved, or whether science is at all close to doing so, you are in the right place. On the outskirts of the city we have a research facility, The Strada Institute, run by a Doctor Margherita Dumas, who is one of the world's leading experts in the field of cloning technology. Go see her, talk to her; I'm sure she'll be only too happy to help. Now for point three. Even if the murdered men were all victims of some clandestine cloning experiment, that doesn't explain why they are suddenly being killed off in rapid succession, and in a particularly singular fashion. It's not every day that a murderer goes to the trouble of ensuring his success by adding poison to the blade of his knife. That, I'm afraid, is where your theory stumbles a little, as, even allowing for the possibility of the clones; that in itself doesn't provide us with a motive for the killings."

"You're right of course, sir," said Houston, "but as yet, my theory is only in its infancy. If we can find out for certain that these men *were* clones, and who brought them into the world, so to speak, then we might be some way along the road to establishing a motive."

"You have a point, inspector," nodded Borgo, "Go, speak to the good Doctor Dumas. See if she can shed some light on the mystery."

An hour later, after a phone call from Borgo had set up a meeting with the head of the Strada Institute, Inspector Harry Houston and Sergeant Debbie Forbes sat opposite the diminutive figure of Doctor Margherita Dumas, heralded as one of the world's leading authorities on the cloning process.

"So you see, inspector," said the doctor after a half-hour consultation with the detectives, "human cloning is a definite possibility, and one that gives us great hope for the future of medical science. Forget the Frankenstein theories of the sceptics. With cloning we can learn so much about life itself, and find new ways to combat diseases, perhaps extend the average human life span. Really, the possibilities are endless."

"Yes, I see, I think," said Houston, "but there's still the chance that someone could bring a criminal mind to bear on the whole process, perhaps raise a whole army of criminal masterminds or murderers with which to achieve some ghastly purpose."

"Oh really, inspector," laughed the doctor. "Now you are entering the world of fantasy. What respectable medical person, or foundation or research facility, would lend itself to such an end, I ask you? The Reproductive Cloning Process, if perfected, can only be for the good of mankind, please believe me."

Houston, having previously asked the doctor questions on the mechanics and technology of cloning, now reached across and took a large brown manila envelope from the proffered hand of his sergeant. Opening it, he removed photographs of the victims of the bizarre series of world-wide killings and slowly laid them out on Dumas's desk, facing the doctor.

"Doctor, if what you say is true, can you please give me your opinion on these?"

Dumas inhaled sharply as she took in the sight of the five murdered men, and a long minute passed before she spoke again. "Do you mean to tell me...?"

"Yes, doctor. Someone somewhere has clearly surpassed your expectations and succeeded in cloning a human being. The mystery is why someone should now be systematically killing every one of them, five so far, absolutely identical in every way, and there may be more for all we know."

Seemingly regaining her composure, Dumas replied. "Ah, but, you see, inspector, they wouldn't be exactly identical, no, not at all, though they might appear so to the untrained or unscientific eye."

187

"Please explain, doctor."

"Well, I'll try to simplify it for you. In reproductive cloning, the DNA containing nucleus of an egg is removed and replaced with the DNA from another cell; in this case it would be that of the person to be cloned. The egg is then stimulated to divide and, after a number of divisions it can be planted into the uterus of a suitable female who would eventually give birth to the cloned individual. However, despite sharing the same nuclear DNA, the original and the copy would have minute differences in what is known as mitochondria, which is another source of DNA."

"But forensic tests showed them all to have identical DNA," interrupted the sergeant.

"Of course they would," replied the doctor. "Only by knowing what to look for and by carrying out some very specific and highly delicate tests could you find those differences, so, to all intents and purposes you and any ordinary medical examiner would think them absolutely identical."

The conversation proceeded along the lines of a question and answer session, with Dumas appearing to freely answer any and all of Houston's questions, though she was of course unaware that the policeman who sat opposite her had a degree in forensic studies and knew quite a bit more than the average police detective about the technicalities of the process she was describing.

At length the doctor asked of Houston, "Do you have any idea who is killing these men, inspector? What could be the possible motive for such a crime?

"As yet we have no suspects, doctor, and few real clues to go on. I'd like to ask you one last question before we go, if I may?"

"But of course," Dumas replied.

"You, Doctor Dumas, are one of the world's leading authorities on the cloning process, but, do you know of anyone who may have been involved in such research thirty years ago, and who may be responsible for the births of the five dead men? In particular, do you know of anyone who may have been prepared to conduct unethical experiments in order to achieve some sort of fame within the profession?"

"Now, really, inspector, do you seriously believe that anyone in my profession would risk their reputation and their career on such a thing? I know of no one now or then who would have been prepared to take such a risk. I really don't think I can help you any more. Now, if you don't mind?"

Dumas simply nodded at them as the detectives rose and moved towards the door on their way out. The interview was over.

Chapter Forty-Two

On the drive back into the city a while later, the two police officers discussed their meeting with the doctor.

"Did you see her face when you showed her the photos?" asked Forbes with a grin on her face.

"I did indeed, Debs," replied Houston, "but, did you also see how shocked she was, either to know they were all dead, or to know that the police forces of the world had realised that something to do with cloning is going on? That was the kind of shock that registers when a person is told of or sees a picture of someone they *know* who's died. I think we need to look at the good Doctor Dumas a little more closely, Sergeant Forbes."

"You're right, sir, and I've just thought of something else. It didn't register at the time, but you know on the wall behind her desk? Well, there was a series of photographs displayed there. I assumed they were family, or maybe former patients. There was one missing in the middle row, near the end on her left. Now, why do you think that might be sir?"

"Why indeed, Debs, why indeed? Perhaps we'll pay our friend Commissioner Borgo another visit in the morning," mused the inspector as they arrived at their hotel.

At nine-thirty on Tuesday morning, the two Scottish officers found themselves once again in the office of Commissioner Borgo. Having checked in with the rest of the team via Houston's laptop and having been informed that there was no progress to report in Milan, London, Aberdeen, or New York, they were eager to pursue what they thought could be a live avenue of inquiry.

"Doctor Dumas? You are surely joking!" Borgo grinned widely. "Margherita Dumas is one of the most respected scientists in her field, inspector. You cannot honestly believe that she is somehow involved in all of this."

"As you say, sir, she is one of the leading experts in the science of cloning. Who better to have developed a successful process and perhaps tested it in secret, a sort of long-term research and development process?"

"So you expect me to believe that she developed a successful human cloning programme over thirty years ago, and brought an unknown number of clones into existence, and now somehow she's having them all killed? I think, Inspector Houston, that you are stretching credibility too far, based on little if any evidence. A missing picture? A look on her face? Ha! Preposterous, really."

"Not as preposterous as you may think, sir," chimed Debbie Forbes, "I did a little checking, and it seems that Doctor Dumas set up the Strada Institute twenty-five years ago with a massive grant from the International Human Embryology Research Foundation, based on her far-reaching and futuristic theories relating to the cloning of human beings. At the time the subject was one that was surrounded by controversy and taboo, and she had few supporters outside the clinical science fraternity. Prior to her research into cloning, she was actively involved in a fertility clinic in Brussels, which itself was regarded as a pioneer in the field of the treatment of infertility in women. Her success rate was more than double that of any other clinic of its kind. That clinic was burned to the ground by a mysterious fire, and though no evidence was ever produced to confirm it, arson was suspected at the time. It's possible the clinic may have been deliberately destroyed in order to destroy evidence of cloning experiments."

Though still very doubtful, Borgo authorised a check on the history of the Strada Institute, and also ordered his team to dig into the background of the clinic she'd funded in Brussels. Co-operation was sought and gained from the Belgian police, and another link was added to the international chain of investigation.

Houston meanwhile ordered his team to check the backgrounds of the murdered men. The connection with the fertility clinic had raised a spectre of an idea in his mind, and he needed to check it out. Debbie Forbes headed back to Aberdeen to co-ordinate the Scottish end of the investigation with Boyd, McNally, Forester, and Dunblane with her trusty computer, and would report to Houston with the findings of the investigation into the personal lives of the victims, with specific attention being given to the mothers of the murdered men.

Two days later, she reported to her boss with the preliminary results. Like Forbes, Houston was stunned to discover that the murdered men's mothers had all paid a visit to the Sobel Clinic in Brussels thirty years ago! All had become pregnant after receiving a pioneering treatment developed by Doctor Margherita Dumas, and administered by the clinic's director, a Doctor Alexander Renaud. Even more interesting was the fact that Renaud had died in suspicious circumstances just a few weeks ago, having apparently fallen over the parapet of a bridge into the river near his home. Renaud had at one time been an Olympic standard swimmer, and despite having been in his sixties at the time of his death, it had been thought odd that he could have drowned in a shallow and slow-moving river. The fall from the bridge was not a long one, and there was no evidence that he had hit his head on the brickwork of the bridge on the way down, which might have caused him to lose consciousness and impeded his ability to swim to the bank. Though foul play had been suspected, it was inevitable in the light of the evidence (or rather the lack of it), that a verdict of death by misadventure was returned by the presiding magistrate at the inquest into his death.

Houston now felt that they were getting somewhere, though the motive for the murders was still a mystery to him. Commissioner Borgo had begun to believe in the wild theory propounded by the Scottish detective, and offered his full co-operation. As the Swiss homicide squad began their investigation into the activities of Doctor Dumas and her institute, Sergeant Debbie Forbes provided her boss with the most vital piece of evidence so far. In an excited phone call from Grampian police headquarters in Aberdeen, she almost shouted down the phone, "Sir, take a look at the photo I've just e-mailed to your laptop. You should have it now."

Houston opened up his laptop and accessed his incoming e-mail. Sure enough, there was a photo file waiting to be opened. As he saw the face that came into view on his screen, the inspector was incredulous.

"But Debs, "he spoke into the phone, "that's… that's… it has to be…."

"That sir," she said with a sense of grim satisfaction, "is Doctor Alexander Renaud, taken a few months before his death, and as you so rightly deduce, the good doctor looks like an older but identical version of the murdered men. I think we can safely say that we've found the prototype for Doctor Dumas's cloning experiment, the cell donor, or whatever they call it."

"So, she did do it, she cloned a human being, and not just once either, and Renaud was in it with her."

"There's more sir. Our contacts in Belgium have come up with the surprising fact that the brilliant Doctor Dumas was at one time rumoured to have given birth to a child, though no one seems to know what became of it. It was just a rumour, as I've said. No births were ever registered, but a member of staff who worked at the institute when it first opened swears that she was pregnant at the time, and was then absent for months, and he thought it was because she'd given birth to a child. No one had the guts to ask her about it though, as she'd never volunteered any information, not even to tell her employees she was expecting a child, so they respected her privacy by not mentioning it. Some later thought she'd miscarried and just didn't want to talk about it."

"I'm getting a whole new picture of our good Doctor Dumas," said Houston, "and I've got another idea. I want you on the next flight over here, Debs, and we're going to pay a call on the lady again."

"Right sir, I'll be with you as soon as I can get there. Can I ask you what you're proposing?"

"Patience, sergeant, patience," replied Houston, with a hint of conspiratorial silence in his voice.

Debbie Forbes knew him well enough not to question him further. She knew that he'd reveal his thoughts and tactics to her when he was good and ready. She left the office an hour later and returned to her flat on George Street in the city, staying just long enough to pack her case with fresh clothes and toiletries. Houston hadn't given her any indication of how long she'd be with him in Zurich, so she packed enough for a week's stay, just in case. Mary Dunblane had reserved her a seat on the next flight from Edinburgh to Zurich, there being no flights scheduled from Aberdeen, and she called a taxi, and was soon on her way to the railway station where she boarded the train to Edinburgh and less than three hours later she was in the air, winging her way to what she hoped might be the solution to a mystery that was baffling police forces around the world.

At eleven the next morning, Houston and Forbes, accompanied by Karl Faucus of the Zurich homicide team, paid an unannounced visit to the Strada Institute, Houston not wanting to give the doctor any warning of his arrival, and thus the opportunity to remove or destroy the evidence he hoped to find. He'd briefed Debbie Forbes over dinner at the hotel the night before, and she was fully aware of her boss's theory and his intentions that morning. Houston had also consulted with Commissioner Borgo, who had arranged for a support team of officers from his homicide squad to be positioned strategically close to the institute. The leader of the team was in radio contact with Houston.

Dumas's secretary was a formidable obstacle in their attempts to interview the doctor. A large woman with a personality that could only be described as forceful and intimidating, she at first refused to allow the police officers entry to her boss's office. Only when Faucus threatened to arrest her for obstruction did she relent and stand aside to allow the officers entry to Dumas's inner sanctum.

The surprise on Margherita Dumas's face was palpable as the three police officers entered her office unannounced. Her look of surprise however, quickly gave way to one of anger and she spoke to Houston in a tone that was immediately threatening.

"What, may I ask is the meaning of this intrusion? You gave me no warning that you wished to visit my institute again, and here you are barging your way into my office. I've told you all I can about the cloning process, and now you defile my hospitality and co-operation by this unwarranted disturbance. I am a very busy woman and I have much important work to do. Now, please leave, *immediately*!"

"I'm sorry, Doctor Dumas," said Houston, "but we're not going any-where until we get some answers from you. There are certain questions about your past that need clearing up, and I think they have a direct bearing on the series of murders we're investigating."

"Rubbish," shouted Dumas. "What can I possibly tell you that could throw light on the crime of murder? This is a scientific institute, a place of research. We are here to find ways of prolonging human life, not ending it."

"Where is your son, Doctor Dumas?"

The question, coming suddenly from Debbie Forbes completely stunned the doctor, and threw her into a state of visible panic. "Son, what son? I don't have a son," she screeched at Forbes.

"Then who is that in the picture behind you, the one you removed prior to our last visit?"

Forbes had quickly noticed the picture as she'd entered the room, and had been surprised to see that it contained the image of not just one young boy, but two, and they appeared to be identical, twins in fact.

"I, I, well…" stammered the doctor, suddenly at a loss for words.

"You gave birth to twins, didn't you, doctor?" asked Houston, now going fully onto the offensive. "You developed a successful method of human cloning at your clinic in Brussels all those years ago, and you and Alexander Renaud combined his cells and your eggs to produce a child, or in this case two. You then advertised your services as a fertility clinic worldwide, and you used certain of the women who came to you as guinea pigs for your cloning programme. But something went wrong, didn't it, doctor? You found out something that terrified you, horrified you, and you had to take steps to eliminate all traces of your experiments, even down to killing poor Renaud, the father of your human lab rats. Somehow, I think you cajoled your mystery twins into killing for you. They're the ones who've been murdering their siblings around the world. I admit I was puzzled at the speed that our killer was getting around from country to country, locating his victims and then carrying out the crimes, but now I see how easy it was. There wasn't just one killer, there were two! Please correct me if I'm guessing incorrectly won't you, Doctor Dumas?"

Dumas crumpled. She slumped in her chair and assumed the appearance of a defeated woman. She knew that the clever and persistent Scottish detective had learned, or guessed enough to make her position untenable. All her years of deceit, subterfuge, and the string of murders that littered her past now meant nothing, as the realisation was forced upon her that this clever young detective had unravelled almost every thread of the story behind the Nemesis cell and its awful consequences. Perhaps in a last twisted show of defiance, an attempt to prove how clever she had been for so long, and how superior her intellect was when compared with her peers, Dumas took the conscious decision to reveal all, to ensure that Houston realised just what a genius she was, such was the insanity that now found full reign in her mind. Dumas was finished, and she knew it. It was time, as she saw it, to take the curtain call for her work, lest she be denied her moment of revelation by the foolish and the ignorant forces of the law and the justice system which would now be ranged against her in their entirety. She sighed a deep sigh and leaned back in her chair, all trace of her previous belligerence and arrogance gone.

"You are indeed a clever man, inspector," she said, and continued in a crestfallen tone. "For the most part you are correct; though allow me to tell you the whole story. It's true that Renaud and I were working together in Brussels, and that we developed what we thought was a workable cloning method. It was a long time ago and the medical authorities would not have sanctioned our work had they known of it. Much of what we did would have been considered unethical by the standards of the day and maybe still would be today. I won't bore you with the technicalities, but we succeeded in removing cells from Renaud, and implanting them into my eggs, and fertilisation occurred. Division took place though not fast enough and we couldn't produce a viable embryo. That's when we introduced the accelerant."

"Accelerant? What do mean by an accelerant, doctor?" asked Houston.

"In order to produce a viable growing embryo, we introduced an extra DNA strand that had been bombarded with radiation. We had tried numerous ways of achieving our aim, and this one worked. Cell division was rapid, and the fertilised egg began growing at the required rate. We implanted the egg back into my womb, where it somehow divided again and we found that I was in fact expecting twins. It wasn't supposed to happen. We had great concerns about how and why it had happened, but as the pregnancy continued both foetuses seemed to be growing naturally and healthily so we allowed them to go to full-term. They were born thirty-two years ago, inspector, and we called them Alexei and Arturo. They spent their first two years in a sealed environment we created, built to resemble a home, and when we were sure that they were perfectly healthy and normal, we introduced the procedure at the clinic, secretly and on women who had no real hope of ever conceiving a child. The mothers knew nothing about what we'd done and were simply delighted when they later found that our pioneering methods had resulted in them becoming pregnant.

"What we didn't know at the time, and only recently learned was that the accelerant we'd used had produced a serious long-term effect on the clones. The radioactive cell we'd introduced to the foetal DNA had caused a delayed reaction in their metabolism and in their higher brain functions. Soon after they'd reached the age of twenty-six, Alexei and Arturo began to show signs of serious mental stress. Physical symptoms and severe headaches began to manifest themselves, and Renaud and I carried out extensive tests on them both. We were horrified to find that the accelerant had begun a new reaction in their bodies. There was a whole new pattern of cell division taking place, and also a proliferation of new cells was forming in their bodies. They were like a cancer, but not like any cancer the human race has seen up to now. The new cells, we called them the Nemesis cells, were carrying a radioactive charge and were gradually forming tumours in various internal organs. There was even significant activity in the brain, and we knew that something had gone drastically wrong."

"Couldn't you do anything to stop it?" asked Houston, as the doctor paused for breath.

"We tried, we really did," said the doctor, "but the progress of the Nemesis cells was irreversible. We knew, though we didn't tell Alexei and Arturo at first, that they would eventually experience total mental breakdown and massive carcinomas in various parts of their bodies, though we didn't know which would come first. They'd known from a young age that they were different from other people. We'd told them about their conception when we'd felt they were old enough to understand, so we had no problem about them wanting to go to a regular hospital or asking for a second opinion or anything like that. They had been brought up to respond absolutely to my instructions and commands. I knew what I had to do when Renaud started saying that we should get help from outside, reveal what we'd done all those years ago. He thought that we could do something to save the others as well, that we owed it to them to try. I told him that they weren't real people, they were clones, the products of an experiment that had gone wrong, and that they should be terminated, as we would have done with lab rats in the same situation, but he wouldn't listen. He wanted to go to the authorities. He threatened to expose us to the police, the medical ethics commission. It would have ruined us, *me* especially. The institute would have been finished, and all my work would have been for nothing."

Houston and the others could hardly believe what they were hearing. The doctor's words were cold, chilling, and totally devoid of feeling for those lives she had created. No one interrupted, however. The doctor hadn't finished and they didn't want to miss a word of her fascinating and disturbing confession.

"Getting them to dispose of Renaud was easy. When I told them that he was about to expose us, that they'd be taken away from the only home they'd ever known and turned into some sort of medical sideshow and treated as freaks to be experimented on, they were easy to convince. They went to his home town and waited for him to go for one of his regular walks. They stopped him at the bridge and said they wanted to talk to him. Alexei was speaking to him and Arturo walked behind him and used a low power stun gun on him to render him unconscious. Then they simply threw him into the river. He would have drowned before the water could revive him.

"They knew we had to get rid of the others as well before the Nemesis cells began their work. I had convinced them that we would all be in danger if anyone ever discovered the truth. Tracing the others was easy, of course, as I'd been sending them preventative medications for years. The boys then set about the task of disposing of them. The poison we used made sure that they died as quickly as possible; it was a synthetic derivative of curare. With their deaths, the dormant Nemesis cells would die too, and there would have been no trace of them at autopsy, simply because no one would have been looking for them."

"Where are the boys?" asked Houston, his voice flat and devoid of emotion. He was too amazed and stunned by the doctor's callous tale to feel anything at that moment. "Where are Alexei and Arturo, doctor?"

"Come with me," said Dumas.

A few minutes later they stood staring down at two bronze plaques set into the grass under a large oak tree in the grounds of the institute. The first was inscribed C2476/74, the second C2477/74.

"Doctor Dumas, what are trying to tell me here?" asked Houston.

"Alexei and Arturo are there, inspector. After they'd carried out their task I gave them both large doses of sedatives one night followed by a larger dose of the curare derivative. They died in their sleep, and I cremated them both in the crematorium we have here at the institute for disposing of experimental tissue. Those numbers are their serial numbers, the number of the experiment they each represented. I thought no one would ever find out what had really happened, that I'd destroyed all the evidence. It seems I was wrong."

As they left the institute that day with the doctor in handcuffs, the detectives couldn't help but be completely appalled and saddened by Dumas's lack of humanity. Even in death she had thought of the two young men who'd probably looked upon her as their mother as nothing more than a pair of laboratory specimens, callously despatching them when they'd fulfilled their purpose. They were an experiment gone wrong to her, nothing more, and they'd been disposed of and cremated, and their ashes buried without a name, just an experiment number as their only memorial. They may have wielded the knife but Dumas was, in the detectives' minds, the real killer of all those who had tragically died in the name of her scientific aspirations.

* * *

Doctor Margherita Dumas never stood trial for the murders of Alexei and Arturo, or any of the other victims. Extensive psychological and psychiatric examinations were carried out, and she was declared mentally unfit to plead. She was ordered to be detained indefinitely in Switzerland's largest and most secure psychiatric unit, where she languishes to this day. The medical ethics authorities decided that there was nothing positive to be gained by making public disclosure of her ghastly Genesis experiments, or the resulting Nemesis cells, and it was agreed to keep all information regarding her work a closely guarded secret.

Harry Houston and Debbie Forbes returned home to Scotland, where the special task force set up to investigate the murders of the clones, as the police later referred to the case, was stood down. Around the world the various police forces that had been involved in the case closed their files. All loose ends were considered to have been tied up. It had never been public knowledge that the victims around the world were identical, and each police force was able to present a valid solution for the murders in their own countries, enabling the medical profession to keep their secrets. Where it was deemed necessary, news was released to the press and public that the murderer of a particular victim was an unknown assailant with an equally unknown motive, not perfect of course, but it enabled the Frankenstein scenario raised by Dumas to be kept from the public, who were deemed not to need to know that a doctor of Dumas's reputation and standing had managed to play God all those years ago, and had come close to succeeding. Gradually Doctor Margherita Dumas and her Nemesis cell faded into the memory of those involved.

Brussels, Friday the 13th September, 2006

At the home of the deceased Doctor Alexander Renaud, his widow Marlette heard the front door opening, and rushed to greet her visitor. "David, my darling," she cried," It's so good to see you; I can't tell you how much I've missed you."

"I'm so sorry I missed the funeral, Mother, I'd never have left to go backpacking around the world if I'd known what was going to happen. If only I'd phoned home sooner, before I reached Australia. I only knew about Father's death a fortnight ago, when your letter caught up with me through the student union. I couldn't believe it when you told me what had happened. I got back as soon as I could."

"I know, my son, I know," said Marlette as the tears ran down her face both with the continued grief at the loss of her husband, and the relief of having her big strapping twenty-six year old son home again. He was her pride and joy, conceived with the help of Alexander's knowledge of infertility treatments after she'd had trouble conceiving naturally. Only Renaud ever knew what had happened to the sixth Nemesis cell, originally intended for the Polish girl, Christa.

"Now, tell me my son, how have you been?"

"Well, Mother," he replied, "I've been having these terrible headaches lately…"

Dear reader,

We hope you enjoyed reading *The Nemesis Cell.* Please take a moment to leave a review, even if it's a short one. Your opinion is important to us.

Discover more books by Brian L Porter at https://www.nextchapter.pub/authors/brian-porter-mystery-author-liverpool-united-kingdom

Want to know when one of our books is free or discounted? Join the newsletter at http://eepurl.com/bqqB3H

Best regards,
Brian L Porter and the Next Chapter Team

About the Author

Winner, Best Author, The Preditors & Editors Readers Awards 2009, and also Winner of Best Children's Book, and Best Artwork for *'Tilly's Tale'* (under his Harry Porter pseudonym), and with a Top Ten Finisher Award for his thriller *'Legacy of the Ripper'*, Brian L Porter is the author of a number of successful novels. His works include the winner of The Preditors & Editors Best Thriller Novel 2008 Award, *A Study in Red – The Secret Journal of Jack the Ripper* and its sequels, *Legacy of the Ripper* and the final part of his Ripper trilogy, *Requiem for the Ripper*, all signed for movie adaptation by Thunderball Films (L.A.), with *A Study in Red* already in the development stages of production. Both *A Study in Red* and *Legacy of the Ripper* were awarded 'Recommended Read' status by the reviewers at CK2S Kwips & Kritiques.

Aside from his works on Jack the Ripper his other works include *Pestilence, Purple Death, Glastonbury, Kiss of Life* and *The Nemesis Cell*, and the short story collection, *The Voice of Anton Bouchard and Other Stories*.

Next Chapter is pleased to have been able to publish new, second editions of *Behind Closed Doors* and *Purple Death*, in addition to this new edition of *The Nemesis Cell*, and please look out for the forthcoming *Avenue of the Dead* and new short story compendium, *After Armageddon*.

Brian has also become thoroughly integrated into the movie business since his first involvement with Thunderball Films LLC and is now also an Associate Producer and Co-Producer on a number of developing movies, as well as being a screenwriter for many of the movies soon to be released by Thunderball.

He is a dedicated dog lover and rescuer and he and his wife share their home with a number of rescued dogs.

The Nemesis Cell
ISBN: 978-4-86752-179-3

Published by
Next Chapter
1-60-20 Minami-Otsuka
170-0005 Toshima-Ku, Tokyo
+818035793528
27th July 2021

Lightning Source UK Ltd.
Milton Keynes UK
UKHW010710120821
388748UK00001B/321